Praise for *X in Flight*, Book ...

"Rivers's writing is achingly, hilariously perceptive ... I look forward to seeing what Karen Rivers does with the rest of her planned XYZ trilogy ..." — *Vancouver Sun*

"Rivers integrates [an] element of magic with ease and great naturalness ... This gritty, angst-ridden novel is dark ... but its rather surprising conclusion offers a measure of hope." — *Quill & Quire*

"... [T]he narrative delves into the heart of these three characters, giving each a richness and depth that will resonate ... The voices are authentic and engaging ... teens will be waiting with anticipation for the next book in the 'XYZ Trilogy.'" — *CM Magazine*

Praise for Karen Rivers' Haley Andromeda Trilogy:

The Healing Time of Hickeys
"This book will have you laughing out loud. Haley is a completely loveable and crazy character ... It's guaranteed to make you giggle and feel good — what more could you want in a book?" — *Kidzworld*

"Sixteen-year-old Haley Harmony is ... a likeable, grounded soul, despite the fact that she spends an awful lot of time hyperventilating ... A pleasure from start to finish." — *Quill & Quire*

Y in the Shadows

In the Shadows

Y in the Shadows

BOOK TWO

KAREN RIVERS

RAINCOAST BOOKS
www.raincoast.com

Raincoast Books gratefully acknowledges the financial support of the Province of
British Columbia through the BC Arts Council and the Book Publishing Tax
Credit and the Government of Canada through the Canada Council for the Arts
and the Book Publishing Industry Development Program (BPIDP).

Edited by Colin Thomas
Cover by David Drummond
Interior design by Tannice Goddard
Typesetting by Five Seventeen

NATIONAL LIBRARY OF CANADA CATALOGUING IN PUBLICATION DATA

Rivers, Karen, 1970–
  Y in the shadows / Karen Rivers.
ISBN 13: 978-1-55192-972-9
ISBN 10: 1-55192-972-4
1. Title.
PS8585.I8778Y25 2008   JC813'.54   C2007-9004846-3

LIBRARY OF CONGRESS CONTROL NUMBER: 2007933941

Raincoast Books   *In the United States:*
9050 Shaughnessy Street   Publishers Group West
Vancouver, British Columbia   1700 Fourth Street
Canada V6P 6E5   Berkeley, California
www.raincoast.com   94710

Raincoast Books is committed to protecting the environment and to the
responsible use of natural resources. We are working with suppliers and
printers to phase out our use of paper produced from ancient forests. This
book is printed with vegetable-based inks on 100% ancient-forest-free,
40% post-consumer recycled, processed chlorine- and acid-free paper.
For further information, visit our website at www.raincoast.com/publishing/.

Printed in Canada by Webcom.

10 9 8 7 6 5 4 3 2 1

Every writer has a hero in the shadows — her editor.
This one is for you, Colin. Thank you for helping me to find and
shape the story and for making the words shine.

Yale

1

It started with something unimaginable. Something more like a punchline to a really bad joke than a real possibility, you know? Something that you'd see in some kind of cheesy spoof movie, over-the-top and gut-churningly dumb. And it happened to me. It did. Now when I think about it, it seems surreal. Like a nightmare. It's so overwhelmingly, devastatingly, embarrassingly bad that I can hardly bring myself to tell. It's beyond humiliating. Beyond anything.

"Beyond *beyond*," as someone cooler than me would say, probably mussing her perfectly messy-tidy hair at the same time or coyly covering her mouth with her perfectly subtly manicured hand. She'd be someone totally unlike me. Someone who wears clothes brand new from The Gap or Urban Outfitters or one of a thousand identikit stores, but in mysteriously perfect combinations, and makes them look better than they were ever intended to look. Someone whose shoes always look new even when they aren't. Someone who smells like fresh-cut lilies and cake. Who has teeth so sugar-white you want to pluck them out and crunch them like rock candy. Hands like a bird's wings, you know what I mean? Overly pretty. Fingers like feathers. Sharp sparkling eyes. When she walks, you want to be her hair, the way it's *moving*. When you see her, you want to *know* her. You want her to like you but you can't explain why. It's not like a crush. It's different than that. It's more intense and less meaningful at the same time. It's like hungering after a perfect pair of boots or jeans. It's yearning for something more perfect than what seems real. A different life. A different existence. A different *you*.

See, if Michael Hyde-Smith liked me, then it would mean I was a different person than who I am. As I am now, who would want to know me? My inner strings are so taut that you could probably pluck them and make music. Sometimes my hands tremble like my skin can't quite keep my pulse inside, you know? Like nothing is quite the right fit.

I'm *quirky*. But I don't want to be.

It's how I live my life. Believe me. *Wanting*. Wanting to be someone special, someone smooth as cellophane, pretty in a way that is more than just symmetrical features, in an all-encompassing way. Wanting to shine, easily, without effort. Wanting to be someone else. Someone more.

Someone like Michael.

She's such a bitch, I guess. Popular. Surrounded by girls I can't stand — The Girls — girls so purely evil that I can't believe they can stand themselves. Michael is different, though. Somehow. I don't know why she matters to me, to everyone. But she does. She walks through the halls of the school and heads turn in spite of themselves. Mine does. It always has. Since forever. Since kindergarten, at least, when she showed up in a dress (everyone else in jeans, pants, shorts) and instead of being the odd one, she somehow made us all feel underdressed. It's just how she is. The natural leader, born into it, like royalty.

It's not like I emulate her style or her hair or anything about her. Me and Michael Hyde-Smith, we couldn't be less alike.

I'm not pretty.

Michael is preternaturally, movie-star, straight-up beautiful.

But mostly, she just seems *happier* than the rest of the population. Maybe that's it. All the good hair that slips around like shards of shining metal thread. All the money and good clothes cut to make her body look perfect. That's just the packaging. It's the inside part, that satisfied happiness she gets to wear like it's her right. Her entitlement.

I wanted that so badly. I wanted the kind of life where I *wanted* to go to the prom. Where I knew how to dance, and I liked it. Where I'd make my own dress and I'd look like Gwyneth Paltrow accepting an Oscar, my immaculate blonde hair (as if) flowing to my waist.

Beyond that, I wanted (okay, *still* want, will probably always want) normal things: like a name that doesn't make people stop and look twice, looking confused. Saying, "Uh, Yale? Isn't that, like — is that a *name*? Isn't that a college or something?" (Yes, it is, dumb-ass. My parents went there. They liked it. A little *too* much. Obviously.)

To have eyes that were the same colour as each other. (What a dreamer, huh?) Not one grey-brown and one ice-cold glass blue, silvery, like something too cold to touch. When I was really small, my eye scared me. How unhealthy is that? No wonder I'm wound so tight. Imagine being afraid of *yourself*. I used to think my stuffed animals would freeze if I looked at them too long through that blue lens. I thought the eye was glass, a marble that had somehow fallen in there before I was born, something my mother swallowed that got planted there like a seed and stuck.

If I were a different person, maybe I could make my eyes seem fascinating and mysterious and enticing. Michael would, I'm sure. She *could*. But on me, they are just *too*. Too disturbing, too crazy, too unusual. Too easy to make fun of. Like, "*Wow!* That's ... uh, *wow*. That's really, uh, cool. You're like one of those dogs."

Great.

That's *perfect*.

Just what everyone hopes to hear one day, "You're like ... one of those *dogs*."

It gets worse: I have a tendency to get dizzy and faint. Especially on buses, which is too bad for me because my parents don't drive themselves, so they can't imagine why I would want to do it. They use skateboards or the afore-mentioned horror of public transport — the bus. After I fainted on one for the third time, they "compromised" and got me a scooter that sounds like an ancient environ-mentally hazardous lawnmower trying to cut through gravel and toxic waste. Ironically, it's ostensibly "green-friendly." Planet-saving. A friend to furry animals and green grasses everywhere.

The scooter breaks down almost every time I use it. Usually at an intersection (a busy one). It spurts random clots of black oil onto the road, like an old man spitting snot onto the sidewalk. It *horks*. The steering wobbles. The seat creaks and is cracked in such a way that, if I wear shorts, it grabs the skin on my thighs and pinches so hard it brings tears to my eyes.

Michael drives a brand new Jeep Liberty, bright red and shiny. Leather seats. Stereo system. Sunroof.

My scooter is a dull army green.

So, yeah. That pretty much sums up my life, so far. I'm the tiny girl who doesn't have good hair, doesn't have good friends, doesn't have that magic whatever, the sparkle and the fun. Dog's eyes, hands aquiver, heart beating like something is always just about to happen, hair that just lies flat. A laugh like something barking. A voice like a lifelong smoker, even though I only started last year, and I only ever smoke the clove ones. Chronic dark bags framing my creepy eyes. The most humiliating means of transportation known to man.

You get what you get, my mum says. Don't ask for more. Life hands you what you can handle.

My mum is one of *those* people. I guess she considers herself Zen. *Deeply* thoughtful. She has all those books, you know. Like *The Tao of Pooh*. One philosophy after another, all some easy-to-swallow variation on Buddhist acceptance and finding inner peace. Honestly, everything about this makes me furious: if you're going to be Zen, at least read the real books. Read something that's never been on the *New York Times* bestseller list. That's not philosophy, it's beach reading. But she doesn't go in much for the big books, the real heavies. Keep in mind, she smokes a lot of pot. Surely it's that and not the dumb philosophies that takes the edge off, helps her find some kind of peace, inner or otherwise. Pot stinks. I hate that she and Dad do that, huddled over their computers, giggling like kids. It makes me mad. It makes me want to slap them and shout, "You aren't making sense! You're rambling!"

Well, you get what you get.

Until the weirdness started, I thought what I got wasn't a lot of anything. Not a lot of friends, that's for sure. Not *one* person to call my BFF — a phrase, for the record, that makes me want to stick a fork in my eye. Best Friends Forever? Please. But still, I want to be able to say that about someone, anyone. Not even Michael, just someone who would *get* me. Someone who I wouldn't feel like I was boring them to death with my stuff. I try. Maybe I try too hard? Or I used to. Now I don't bother as much. Once in a while, maybe. But not often. For obvious reasons.

Like last week, for example, I went to the mall with this girl, Anika, from my math class. She's a bit of an oddball, but she's okay. She's smart. She reads. And she's also sort of cool, like she's accepted into any group because she's too unique to fit into any specific one. I would like to be her friend, I guess, if it were an option. Sometimes she wears stripy knee socks like a roller skater from the seventies. Like Michael, she can somehow do that thing where she makes something out-of-the-ordinary look trendy, makes you want to wear those ugly socks too, even though you know it would simply make you look stupid and awkward, like you were wearing a Halloween costume on the wrong day.

She listens to old music, like ABBA and the Bee Gees, and she doesn't care what people think of that. Her nails are all painted different colours, yellow, red, orange, blue, green. She shops at thrift stores and makes her own perfume out of flowers she finds in her yard.

Usually Anika makes me sneeze. She reeks of dandelions. Ragweed.

Anyway, we'd had a detention. Actually the detention was mostly a mistake. She had been horsing around with Aurelia, who *is* Michael's BFF. Aurelia is the bitchiest of The Girls by far, so bitchy she's actually scary. The pitch of her laugh is like the ear-jarring sound you make when you rub your finger around the rim of your glass. It sounds cruel. She's something else. When she talks, she always flings her arms around as if her voice isn't enough to say whatever she's saying, she needs more. So there she was in health class, gesticulating like a nasty headless chicken, and she accidentally (or not) flicked her long pale pink fingernail in the direction of my face and hit me directly in my blue eye. Hard.

For a second, all I could see was red. Then I screamed, but only a little bit. More like a yelp really. Who wouldn't yelp when they got hit in the eye?

Mr. Dixon turned around and Anika was laughing and I was shrieking, so we got it. Aurelia was still as stone, staring down at her paper like studying was her life. She does "fake" so well, it's hard to imagine that anything about her is real.

The thing was, I didn't mind so much. It sort of made us bond, me and Anika. The detention, that is. Mr. Dixon made us play chess as our punishment, which is a game I secretly love. We didn't really play, though; we sort of just pushed the pieces around and rolled our eyes. Oh God, and then Mr. Dixon sneezed and a huge gob of stuff hung, unnoticed, from his nose for ages before it finally dropped onto his sweater. Disgusting. But funny. Really funny.

It seemed like we should do something afterward, almost like we *were* already friends. She wanted to get high but I said I couldn't because of gymnastics. "I'm in training," I said. Which isn't totally true. I mean, they never specifically said we couldn't get high. It's not that kind of training. Not like serious athletics. I just don't *like* drugs, they freak me out. Not in a prudish way, more in a I-bet-if-I-did-that-I'd-die way. (Mum says I'm a fatalist, but I like to think of myself as a realist.) (People do die from drugs, you know, I'm not making it up.) Besides, getting high is my parents' thing. Not mine. I'm rebellious that way.

I suggested the mall instead. I had this idea that we'd try on clothes or get makeovers or hang out in the food court and flirt with the cute guys at the Orange Julius counter or something.

I don't know what I thought.

Life isn't TV, you know?

We bought coffee at Starbucks that tasted terrible: expensive and burnt and, frankly, really gross. (I hate coffee. It makes me feel like my heart is pulled taut, like it might burst like the skin of an overripe fruit.) I tried to remember to breathe. We hung out at the arcade, watching the younger kids playing games. There was a lot of yelling, flashing lights, the zip-zap of the sound started to hurt my ears. Then, out of nowhere, she decided to steal a T-shirt. The disabled guy who ran the kiosk looked sad around his eyes. She asked him for change for a dollar, and he gave it to her, even though there was a sign that said, WE MAKE NO CHANGE. She stuffed the shirt into my gym bag, which I had slung over my shoulder, before I realized what was happening.

Something about hanging around with her made me feel like I was getting the flu, or maybe it was the coffee. She talked too close and so fast I started to feel like I didn't understand the language. Nothing was funny. Her breath made me queasy, made me want to go home and read a book. I was in the middle of *Anna Karenina*. It's deadly boring but somehow relaxing. It takes so long for something to happen that I feel like reading it is the same as being asleep, a slow dream.

I wanted that.

Not the stealing. Not the sad-eyed guy.

Anika hasn't actually talked to me since, except to ask for her stolen shirt. It didn't even fit her. It made her skin look yellow and showed off her belly-overhang bulge. On the front it said, PEOPLE DON'T KILL PEOPLE. ROBOTS KILL PEOPLE. I don't even get that. Is that funny?

You get what you get. Some people get happy and shiny. The only shiny in my life is my nose after a day of sitting under the soul-draining fluorescent lights at Immaculate Conception High. Which only draws attention to whatever zit happens to have formed there when I was looking down at my textbook or staring at the back of Tony Nelson's head. His skin is amazing. Incredible. It's like velvet. Such gorgeous skin for a boy. And it smells unbelievable. It's all I can do not to lean forward and just sniff. Weird, huh? I know it.

I also know that if Tony Nelson knew that I thought he was anything special, he'd laugh. He'd tell his friends and they'd write my name and phone number with Sharpies on the bathroom stall doors. They'd find some way to make me into the punchline of a joke.

Like they need to try.

So I *like* him. But it's like the kind of crush you have on people who will never, ever, ever notice you. People who see right through you, but not to your innermost thoughts, just through and out the other side like you aren't there at all. Besides, it's not really a crush on *him*, Tony Nelson. It's more like the kind of crush I have on a lot of people. A crush on a *part* of him. I also have a crush on Israel's eyes (incredibly bottomless deep brown eyes that make it seem like he must understand things that other people don't see) even though I don't like *him*. Not at all. He's too slick, too shiny, too ... scary. But still, his eyes. Matti's laugh (so real, so contagious, so heartfelt that he seems like he must just be happiness in the flesh). Michael's hair. Anika's style. Aurelia's teeth.

In Tony's case, it's just his smell. His skin just *exactly* smells like fresh dirt. Not dirty dirt. More like *earth*. Like when you're a kid and you're helping your mum weed dandelions out of the garden and your hands sink into the wet, damp ground and later, you can smell it on your skin. It smells calm. It smells like being okay. Like breathing.

His neck and T-shirt are usually a bit damp from sweat. You'd think he'd stink, but he doesn't. He moves so fast all the time it's like he's always halfway through a workout, on his way from a run to a game.

I'm too sensitive to smell. It's too important to me. I know that's weird. I can't help it. It's just *there*. Everything smells. You might not notice it, but I do. I read somewhere about people who have an extreme sensitivity to colours, they see colours in the air where there aren't any. I have that, I think, but it's odours instead.

My house smells terrible. It's the most repulsive smell in town, in the world, in the universe, anywhere. You'd think it wouldn't smell bad, at least to me. You'd think it would smell like "home" and give me a warm, safe feeling regardless of its actual scent. But it's bad.

Really bad.

No matter how much I try to clean it (which is hopeless, anyway, because my parents are pigs), the smell pervades. Someone once told me that if you smell something all the time you don't notice it anymore, so that's why people with gross BO don't care or even notice. Yet to me, my house smells like curry, feet, plastic bandages that have been left on too long. And rotting flowers. Wine and smoke. Old milk.

I notice.

I care.

Probably — given my lack of social success and all that's happened — I should become one of those people who never goes out, stays in my house forever, staring out the window at a patch of ever-never-sometimes-changing sky. But I can't *do* that. Because of the smell.

I can't see the sky from my window, anyway. It's blocked by a satellite dish the size of a Volkswagen Beetle.

My parents like technology.

I should say some things about them but I wouldn't know how or where to start. When I describe things, the first thing that comes to me is what they smell like. My parents smell like cigarettes (marijuana) (for obvious reasons), incense (see above) and the kind of sweet-flower lavender soap that is favoured by elderly women named

Elsie or Blanche. And fish. My parents smell like tuna fish. It's hard to know why. They rarely ever eat it.

My parents are very young. They were twenty when I was born, so even though they're in their thirties now, they are like slightly rumpled teenagers with only a smattering of laugh lines and grey hairs. For fun, they play video games. The latest and greatest. Whatever is new. Even those grotesque ones with limbs being torn off and blood spattering the screen. My dad is a world expert at some particular kind of game programming that makes things look real. 3-D. To play, you have to wear this thing over your head that's as big as a breadbox and suffocates me. I hate it. Video games give me motion sickness.

My mum is famous for blogging, which as far as I can tell is just sharing way-too-personal anecdotes with strangers. She blogs about everything: her thoughts, her "philosophies," her politics, her diet, her hair. She blogs about her college experiences. She blogs about *me*, stuff that's too personal to share. She seems unable to have a thought that she doesn't blog about. For some reason, she has a huge following. Thousands of people go to her site every day. She gets paid every time someone clicks on an ad. My mum's internet friends who occasionally make appearances at the house — blog buddies — are usually ten years younger than her and have names like Stargazer and Chiclet.

Sometimes I feel a bit like I *own* Mum and Dad, like some people have pairs of matching dogs. I feed them and clean up after them and remind them to go outside sometimes so that they get fresh air. They barely notice me, but sometimes they touch me affectionately, pour attention on me for fifteen minutes, and then instantly forget my existence again. It's hard to explain. It's as if all those computers have made them forget how to act for real.

Here is the biggest thing I know about my parents. I don't want to know it because I don't know what to do with it. Knowing it is like knowing I have a tumour somewhere in my body that's growing and growing and growing and it will one day take me over entirely.

Ready?

Before I was born, there was Yale. Not the school (although there was that, too), another human Yale. A baby. My *sister*, I guess, although it's hard to imagine a sister you've never known. How could I ever have known her? Or about her? Here's the bad part, the unbelievable terrible truth: they gave her away. And they never said a word about her, not to me. Not ever.

To make it worse, I read about Yale — found out about her — on Mum's *blog*. Otherwise I wonder if I'd ever have known. I didn't save the entry or anything. I guess it's probably still there, lurking around in cyberspace, if I wanted to go look for it. Which I don't. I don't remember Mum's exact words, but she'd been posting about babies. Childbirth. Someone she knew was having a baby and she was talking about *epidurals*, of all things. Talking about being numb. Well, she must have been, that's all I can say. How could she give away a *baby*? She mentioned Yale in passing, in that context, like she didn't matter. Like she was a pair of shoes that was returned to the store or an umbrella forgotten on the subway.

I keep wanting to ask them about her. About Yale. And about me. What made them keep me if she wasn't good enough? Am I measuring up? See, I doubt that I could be. I'm nothing special. Is she? Did they pick the wrong Yale?

But I can't even broach the subject. If I go to try, it's like my voice box shuts down. My throat closes entirely. My lungs stop moving. But I can't stop thinking about her, wondering what happened. Where *is* she? Is she dead? If so, why is she a secret? Why isn't there even a photo of her on the fridge? Was she adopted? Does she live somewhere not knowing about me, not knowing about us? Does she know?

Every time I talk to them about anything, no matter how weird or trivial, I want to tell them that I know. I *know*. But I don't. I just keep letting it go. It's just always there, in my head, like a quiet black cat quivering on a high shelf, waiting to jump.

I'd be lying if I didn't admit that I avoid my mum now, and her blog. I avoid talking to her because when I do, I'm just reminded of the fact that I'm not talking to her about the only thing I want to talk to her about, and then I feel like I'm letting myself down. And Yale. Crazy, I know. I just ... can't.

Pretty easy to avoid conversations with my parents, anyway. They spend all their time in the basement, where there are about eighty computer terminals, mysterious humming boxes. It smells like burning dust. I don't know how they can stand it. That burning dust smell hurts my nose and scratches up my throat. It makes me gag. But they love it. I hear them laughing down there all the time.

"What's so funny?" I want to yell. "Why are you laughing?"

I don't know what they do, not really. I mean, I know they are programmers, but I can't actually picture what that means. The phone rings in the middle of the night and they have hushed conversations. They rush around looking tired and important. They both wear thick tinted glasses. They work mostly in the half-dark. They sometimes seem to forget who I am. They look at me from behind their identical (on purpose, they buy them in bulk) lenses as though I'm a frog that they've boiled who has mysteriously come back to life.

They weren't there when *it* happened. They rarely came to my meets, even when I wished that they would. Not that I'd ever tell them that. You know.

But, anyway.

It.

Okay. I'm putting off getting started in case it doesn't come out right. In case it just sounds too stupid to be true.

It's a hard story to tell.

Think of the worst thing in the world that's ever happened to you. And I don't mean cancer or having your favourite cousin die in a plane crash or watching your dog being run over by the mailman or having a wild bird pluck out your eye or something gross or epi-tragic. I'm talking about normal-awful. Except not normal.

And *so* awful.

Beyond awful.

Pretend you're me.

You're below-average looking. Maybe you look okay in some light. (The dark, ha ha.) I guess at first glance there is nothing really noticeably grotesque, but there is nothing great either. It's somehow the combination that's wrong. Brown hair with grown-out black lowlights that you can't afford (or be bothered) to fix. Slightly crooked teeth that aren't quite crooked enough to get corrected but crooked enough that you notice. Those dog-like eyes. Skin that's okay in general but usually marred by at least one

zit. Face usually flushed bright red from one embarrassment or another. Very short. Arms almost always
encircled by crooked henna vines that sound much cooler
than they inevitably look. Thin (from all the gymnastics,
the extra hours spent in the gym to avoid going home).
No breasts to speak of (see: gymnastics).

You smell like laundry detergent, something salty, and
pumpkin.

There you are.

You *are* me.

Surprisingly to most people, you're a half-decent gym-
nast. Not even just half-decent. Really good. More than
good. It's a funny talent for you to have; people react to it
like they've suddenly found out that Michael Jordan is a
brilliant poet or that Brad Pitt can ice dance.

You're on the school gymnastics team. You gave up the
non-school stuff, even though they still call from your old
gym and ask you to come back. (It was too far to go to on
the bus and your parents didn't ever seem to remember
when it was time to take you.) The school team sounds
cooler than it is because there are only five of you on the
team and the other four are The Girls — joined at the hip,
the most popular girls in school. The prettiest. The elite.
Sometimes, when you're feeling mean, you think they
share a brain. Mostly, you just want them to like you.
Michael is the leader of the group. It's not something
that's spoken, not like she wears a jacket with a Head Girl
logo or anything like that. It just happened naturally. I
think it's just because she is who she is. The other girls
(Aurelia, Sam, Madison) are all trying to be like her, but
not quite succeeding. They are too bitchy, too insecure,

too mean. Michael doesn't resort to that. I can't explain the dynamic because I'm not sure I understand it. I just know that I don't think she cares too much about what *they* think of her. But they sure do care what *she* thinks. It's like they vie for her attention somehow, always trying to out-cool one another to be in the spotlight. Only the thing is, they aren't really cool. They're just popular because everyone else is scared of them.

Case in point: they still laugh at you behind your back because in the third grade you peed your pants at Samantha Farraday's birthday party. Or because at the one party they dragged you along to last year, you played drinking games and didn't notice the drunkenness creeping up on you until you opened your mouth to say something and threw up on Matti Koivu's lap.

In spite of that, they are, sort of, your friends. They *act* like they like you (sometimes) because you're good enough to sometimes win ribbons at meets. They just don't invite you to parties anymore. You guess you could just show up, but you'd never do that. You'd need to be coerced. Wanted.

Your best event is the uneven bars, your favourite, flying through the air, your hands dusty from chalk and sweat. When you're up there, you aren't really you, awkward blushing quivering *you*. You're someone else.

It doesn't matter now.

Those girls were apparently not good enough friends *not* to stand around laughing at the biggest meet of the year as you're twirling around the bars wondering why the audience is so quiet, and then, halfway through a move where you're forced to look at your own crotch, you see it. *It*. The thing that will make your school life unimaginably horrible. It will make you the butt of all jokes for the rest of the twelfth grade.

You got your *period*.

It.

Your bright red, humiliating, spreading, staining period. In a big way, not just a tiny unnoticeable drop.

In a flood.

Your uniform, of course, is white.

Oh my God, oh my God, oh my God, is all you can say, over and over again, in your head, while it's happening. Your head is going to explode. The gym floor will crack open and swallow you, any second, please let it, only it doesn't, no matter how much you want it — need it — to happen.

And then … well, then it all gets so strange that it's like no one can notice it, it's too far beyond their ability to understand it.

You drop down from the bars, your hands releasing as though they never knew how to hold on in the first place. You fall onto the crash pad. Blushing so furiously red that your face is sweating, burning. You think you might combust. People do. You've read it in a book. You think you smell the smoke of burning, something worse. You think, *okay*, burn. You think, *I have to get out of myself. I have to get away. I have to disappear. I have to disappear. I have to disappear.*

And you do.

It feels like fire. Your skin feels too hot to exist and then suddenly cold. You can't hear or smell anything for a second. Then it comes back in a rush, like static, but heightened. Overwhelming.

But you aren't there. No one can see you. For all intents and purposes, you are *gone*.

Picture it.

Imagine it.

It.

That's how it happened.

I just faded away. I couldn't see my hands.

Wait, that's not totally true. I could see a bit of my hands, a vague outline, an impression of moving light, like sunlight seen from underwater. I was there, but not there. I was hazy, like a watermark or smoke trying to form a shape. At first, I wasn't sure if it was only something to do with my eyes, my vision going bad, blind from maximized, intolerable embarrassment. But I could see everything else.

There was a silence in the gym then. It was so almost-funny. Like a toddler's game: I can see you, but you can't see me. The hush and stillness and people looking around vaguely, at one another, forgetting in that instant because it didn't make sense. There was a smattering of talk and laughter. People shifting and coughing. Someone cat-called, but what they were cat-calling wasn't clear. Me?

But it couldn't have been me. I was gone.

I walked away. I could see the imprint of my feet on the soft mats, but no one else seemed to be looking. Everything seemed louder than usual, clanging in my ears. The sound of my bare feet echoed on the floor, slap, slap, slap, yet it seemed like only I could hear it. My breathing came in gasps. I was crying. The smell of the chalk and feet and industrial floor cleaner was choking me.

The door to the change room was open and I went in. The smells changed, but still pummelled me. Newish paint, fruity soap and shampoo from the showers, the thick murky tang of dried sweat. The reek of slightly burning hair from someone's straightening iron. There were four or five girls in there, no one I knew. No one looked up. I waited until they left, and then I went into a stall and fixed myself up, which was completely unnerving because I could see through myself. I changed into my regular clothes: jeans, white T-shirt, brown boots, a glass pendant on a chain that looked like an eye from a distance. As soon as the clothes touched my skin, they faded to transparencies. I threw my bodysuit into a toilet and flushed, knowing that it would jam and over-flow and flood. It did. I sat there for a few minutes listening to the toilet struggling. It seemed only fair.

I bought a Coke from the vending machine and drank it. It was ice cold and sweet and the bubbles flirted on my tongue. It was delicious. I think it's the best thing I've ever tasted. My stomach made sounds as the carbonation hit. By the time my hands had stopped shaking and my heart had slowed to normal, I was back. There I was, in the mirror. Me. Blurring into focus, ice cold and then warm. My face blotchy from crying, but also pale as paper, as though all the blushing sapped the colour from my flesh.

When I look back on the day, it's funny what I remember the most clearly. I remember in such detail what happened *after*. But the build-up to it, the before, I don't know. It seems both like I'm remembering it wrong and like I can't remember it at all. Like a movie I saw, then dreamed about, and then couldn't distinguish the dream from the movie itself.

I remember the start of a dull aching cramp. Was I bloated? Why didn't I notice? Maybe I'm remembering now symptoms that weren't there. But they must have been. I must have known. I should have known.

I definitely remember that I was hungry. That the weather was just starting to crack open and become warm, although it was raining. I remember the sweaty smell that wet concrete gets when it's warmed by the sun.

The rest has all faded away. When I try to remember more details, it's like I somehow remember fewer of them.

Did it really happen?

Yes.

I do know there was a crowd of staring faces. Then there was hunger. And then, the vanishing.

I guess that's how my story starts, then. I guess that's when everything changed.

TONY

2

THIS MORNING I found out that Dad is leaving again. Bye, Dad. You miserable old jerk. Get out. Go. Take your ugly sweaters with you and your stupid soggy cigars. Your old leather jacket from high school with the cracking sleeves.

It's fine.

I don't care.

Asshole.

Sometimes I half wonder where he goes, but then I don't. I tell myself I don't care and I believe it.

I bet he goes to *his* mother's house, lies in his old room, looks at old pictures of himself as the big high school hero. Whacks off on his perfectly made bed (he'd never make it himself) while remembering the "good old days." Eats Grandma's strange tinned food and lies about how great it is. Lets her do his laundry but bitches at her if she shrinks his shirts. Forgets that he's an adult now and it's not Grandma's job anymore to pick up after him. Forgets how to be anything but an oversized teenager, picking his nose in front of the TV, waiting for her to remind him to go to bed.

I can't imagine him actually going somewhere alone and fending for himself. A hotel or anywhere like that seems impossible. Coping with the check-in process, finding his room, getting his own food. He'd probably die. Besides, who would pick out his shirt and tie?

When he's here, it's terrible.

It's like the worst dark storm only the weather is inside the house, all around him. It's probably not his fault; it's just the way it is. The way he deals, or doesn't deal. The way he percolates. The thunderstorm pressure of him makes me want to go to sleep. I like to lie in my room and read and avoid the other rooms when he might be in them. It's hard to explain *why* exactly because he's not really doing anything wrong.

He doesn't really *do* anything.

He makes dumb comments. He calls me "Bud" and acts like he's my best friend. He sends me crappy e-mail jokes and thinks he knows what I'm all about. He watches reality TV and acts like all the people on the show are his friends. He's probably the only man in the world who reads the *National Enquirer* and thinks it's the same as keeping up with the news. He invites me on crazy weekend trips with his dumber-than-dumb friends to shoot deer or moose or some other poor stupid animal that I'd never kill in a billion years.

I never go.

He's just such a buffoon.

Not like I'm a mental giant or anything, but still. I'm smarter than him.

When I'm in my room, avoiding him, I do weird things. Embarrassing things. And I don't mean like jerking off or sneaking a cigarette. I mean, like I sometimes do science experiments from this kit that I got for Christmas when I was little. Put baking soda into beakers, add funny coloured chemicals, watch it boil over. It's got a microscope. Sometimes I'll find spiders or flies or other gross insects dried up on windowsills in the house and just look at them.

I don't know why I like that. It's a kit for little kids.

I read a lot of comic books. Embarrassing. They aren't just comic books. I guess they're really porn. But dumb porn. Surreal porn. I'd never tell *anyone*. What's worse, never reading or reading comics with naked girls in them?

Both of them seem like things stupid people would like. I don't want to be a buffoon like my dad, but I am probably doomed to be by my genes. I got his eyes, why not his other, less appealing, qualities?

When he's not here, it's worse. It's like the eye of the storm. It's like an illusion of calm. But then it bubbles up again in the form of Mum worrying herself into a frenzy about where he is. She worries if he's ever coming back. She worries that he is.

Mum is a worrier. If she could be a worrier for a living, we'd be fine. She'd be the best worrier the world has ever seen.

I don't care what he does. Dad, that is. You can't pick your parents. You just have to get through it until you are too old to care anymore. Until you've flown the coop.

Later, after school, I'm going to take my basketball down to that old park behind the bowling alley. When we were kids, we always had birthday parties at that bowling alley. Cake and soda and stomach aches and some kid getting his fingers trapped between the balls coming up the ball return. It was a long time ago. Bowling is kind of not what we do now. Trust me.

Maybe as a joke, I guess. Maybe if everyone was baked.

When I head down there to shoot hoops, usually no one else is there except for some homeless dude who stores his shopping cart full of empty bottles in the corner. I call him Hank because he doesn't talk and doesn't exactly wear a name tag saying HELLO, MY NAME IS _____. Calling him Hank makes him seem more human. I'll take him a few empty bottles. No skin off my nose. It's like I pay to play, you know?

The park is so old and underused that the basket is just a hoop with a bunch of old string and rusty chain hanging from it. The paint lines on the court have all been worn away. You have to watch for broken glass. A lot of the surrounding shrubbery is growing into the court so you have to be careful of the blackberry brambles. They haven't flowered yet, the blackberries, that's still months away, but the brambles are already full and green and choking and, believe me, they're sharp. My arms are all scratched up from trying to get the ball back. You have to handle those brambles carefully.

I'm going to shoot exactly one hundred baskets, and then I won't care about my dad.

I'm going to shoot a thousand baskets.

I wonder how long it would take to shoot a million baskets. I don't think I have that kind of time.

Lately I have a weird thing about numbers. I'd never tell anyone. I don't know when it started, but it seemed like one day I started to count everything and what it added up to seemed to matter. I can't explain.

I like even numbers. Sometimes when I'm freaking out about my mum or mad at my dad or whatever, I go for long runs and it just is natural to count my steps. I know it's crazy but it makes me calm the fuck down. I have to make the last step an even number that's all lined up. Like eight hundred and eighty-eight. Two thousand two hundred and twenty-two.

Ever since Joe died ... that's my brother, he died last year.

Died.

I still can't believe it. It doesn't seem real.

Anyway, ever since then, it's all messed up. Dad and Mum can't be in the same room; there isn't enough space for both of them in this house or in this city or on this planet. It's his fault, it's her fault, it's both of their faults; it has to be *someone's* fault. I could close my eyes and imagine the force of their hate for each other propelling them off the sides of the earth, out into space, their faces all shocked and surprised to find out the ground isn't under them any more.

Yeah, it sucks that Joe died. It's the worst thing. It's inconceivable. It can't be true.

And let's not overlook the fact that he *chose* it. It's something he did to us. It didn't just happen. The asshole. Jerk. Idiot.

I'm so *mad*.

I didn't know it was possible to feel this angry.

I feel like ...

I feel like he changed me. I used to be easygoing. Everyone said it. Even my parents. Even Joe.

Then he started with all the drugs. Drugs, drugs, drugs. I don't know what he started with, but by the end it was tons of ecstasy and crystal meth. That was what got him the worst, I think. I don't know what else he did. Other shit I wouldn't know if I stumbled on it, that's for sure. His eyes started to look weird, crazy, blank. They drifted and jerked, like too much caffeine and too much energy. He darted around, and then he slept. For days. Like he was in a coma. Unmoving. When I think about all the times I saw him asleep and thought he was dead, it makes me dizzy. Because now he is.

Dead.

For real. Forever.

All he ever talked about, when he did talk, was insane craziness. He thought he was an artist. A musician. But then he made "statements" by making no art, no music. He spent all his time at raves, gulping down life like it was running out, moving like he had to stay in motion to keep living. He took me once and I hated it. It was too much sound, you know? Like the beat of the music was trying to take over my heartbeat, it made me feel like something else was taking me over. Scared me.

He slept with a pacifier in his mouth like a baby. He was the most frantic and tired kid you ever saw. He made *me* tired. He was always talking so fast and seemed so desperate. He died because he wanted it so badly he couldn't do anything else. I've never known someone whose whole self was such a black hole. A bottomless endless pit of black. Being around him in the last months before he died felt heavy, like trying to breathe underwater.

I guess he got that from Dad. I feel like that about Dad now. But for different reasons. Dad's not on drugs; he's just stuck in some time of his life that doesn't exist any more than Joe exists.

Sometimes I have nightmares about Joe. Sometimes I dream that I'm punching him in the head. Kicking him. Washing off the stupid makeup he used to wear sometimes. Forcing him to dress in something other than leather. Hurting him. I know that's wrong, it probably means I'm as much of an asshole as he was. Maybe I'm the psycho. Maybe he was just mixed up and made a mistake.

If I shoot a thousand baskets, in a row, without missing, everything will be okay. Mum will stop calling in sick to work. She almost got fired from The Bank for crying. She's on some kind of probation now. She told me about it but I couldn't really concentrate. Sometimes I just can't hear her; it's like my ears are full of water.

How can you fire someone for crying? Now she just calls in sick every other day or gets sent home. She lies on the couch in her pink, fluffy, coffee-stained, dog-eared robe sobbing like if she does it hard enough, she'll be done and it will be finished with.

She's something important at The Bank. Her job apparently matters. Vice President of Rich Assholes or something. But she can't stop the tears. I guess it sucks when they are buying and selling countries or customers or whatever they do and suddenly she starts weeping. I want her to stop and just breathe. I want her to be normal. Fuck. *I* want to be normal. I want a normal life. I want to get away from all of this freakiness and all this tripping.

Fuck you, Joe.

My ticket out is college, so I hope I pass the biology test in third period. I hope I do *well*, but it's dumb to hope that. I never do well. I just have to pass. My dad says that athletes don't need to be smart.

He was a football star, so I guess that proves it. He's an idiot.

And he's right, in a way. I have letters from three Ivy League schools shoved into the back of my desk drawer. Solicitation letters. Lots of them. They come more and more often now that the season is heating up and the recruiters are starting to show up at regattas. They're looking for rowers, and I've been rowing since I was twelve, which seems like forever ago. I guess I'm good at it. I should be. I love it; it feels right to me. There is something about the feeling of a boat moving fast through the water, cutting through it like a sharp blade, that's just ... well, it's another world. It's peaceful, is what it is. It's like breathing, but so much more intense. So much faster. Like flying.

But am I good enough?

I don't know.

I haven't told Dad. Or Mum. About the letters, that is. Mum would be so thrilled, she'd die on the spot. She'd think I had it made. Then she'd cry because Joe didn't have it made. Because Joe never got a letter from Yale and never would have, even if he'd lived.

And Dad? Dad would be proven right — sports are everything, after all — and he'd like that too much.

The thing is that I don't know if I'll do anything with those schools, if I'll fill out the applications, which are more about erg scores and race points and height and weight than they are about grades.

Even though I love rowing, I just don't know if I deserve it, if that makes sense. If I get to do something that I love as a job, you know? Do I have the right to have a life that's easy for me? Isn't it supposed to be *harder* than this?

The thing with sports is that, no matter how hard you work, it's just entertainment. I think that's why I like it: nothing depends on it. Not really. At the end of a race or a game, no one dies. No one ends up dead.

Death. I can't imagine what that's like, and I can't stop myself from trying to picture it. Is it just nothing or is there something there? How can anyone know? How can we not be scared?

I'm not Joey. I don't do his kind of drugs.

I am okay without them, without that kind of crazy crutch, without that kind of escape. I am okay.

I will be okay.

I'm not careless. I'm tight, taut like a tiger. Tony the Tiger, that's what my mum used to call me. Now she mostly calls me, "Oh, honey." As in, "Oh, honey, I'll be okay." "Oh, honey, your dad really does love you." "Oh, honey, can you fix dinner tonight? I'm just dead on my feet." "Oh, honey, I'm sorry."

I wonder sometimes about other kids' lives. My best friend, Israel Santiago, his life is great. He's just enjoying the ride, doing what he wants to do, being who he wants to be. He's so popular it's ridiculous. So I guess I am, too. Popular, that is. Riding his coattails, mostly. Using him to stay cool enough that people don't notice me too much.

It's not like I try to get people to like me, they just do. But I'd be lying if I didn't think it was because of him. Before he showed up at school, I was no one special. I was just Tony, some athletic guy. Popular enough but not like now. Now it's like being famous.

I like it.

I wish I were the kind of person who didn't need that, but I do. So that makes me an asshole, I don't care. Maybe high school *is* the best time of our lives. In which case, I should be doing what I'm doing. Collecting friendships as if a popularity contest will somehow save me from everything bad. Everything that real life is all about.

Israel's magical, he just is. And I don't mean that in a gay way. There's just something about him that draws people in and keeps them. He's almost like an actor who is too good-looking for the part who is just playing a kid in high school. Is plays hockey; he's a forward. He's up early in the morning, totally devoted. He'll be famous one day for it, I know it. He's scary good. I wonder if we'll still be friends when he is, or if he'll just move on. I just think we'll always be friends somehow. We always have been. I don't see why it would change, no matter how different our lives get. But I know we'll do different things. He'll be a hockey star, there's no other option for him. It's who he is.

I won't be.

I think we all probably have something, some scary good thing we can do. Am I scary good at rowing? I don't know. I'm *pretty* good. But somehow it's not like Is and his hockey. It's not just about being good, either, I guess. It's about loving it, and being a star at it. And man does he ever have that going on. And he's obsessed. Knows everything about every hockey player who ever played. Watches every game. Kills himself to get more fit, to get better, to get more accurate, to get to perfect.

He's smart, too. He reads and no one would say that he wasn't cool. No one would tease him for standing up in English class and ripping on *Moby Dick* or whatever. It's like he's exempt from the "smart is lame" rule because he's good-looking and an athlete, an athlete who's going to succeed no matter what.

He's smart, but he's also stupid. He does some really dumb-ass things. Some of our other friends, like Jason and Matti and those guys, they're idiots. They're going nowhere fast, as my mum used to say, when she cared about my friends.

They're not really my friends. I hang with them, but Israel, he's my only real friend. After Joe died, I lived with Israel and his family for three months. My own house just wasn't okay in the aftermath. Mum and Dad were not okay. I guess I wasn't okay either.

Is was *everything* to me then: family, friend, whatever you want to call it. I think he saved my life. He made *me* okay somehow, which is weird because, when I was there, we didn't talk much about Joe. It was just that he made everything seem normal. Not Joe's death, but just everything else. He made it seem like life was going on. And then it did. So I guess he was right. But he has that way; I don't know what it is. He has a way of making you feel better than you are.

The girls go nuts, like he's a star. He's something brighter and more important than everyone else. Nothing makes him stress. He's like liquid. I don't know what I mean by that, but it fits.

His family lives up the street in an identical house to ours but in a completely different life. They laugh all the time. It's light there. Nothing is so serious, not like at home.

Living there was like finally stopping holding my breath. I can't explain really. It's just that they are so *easy*.

They eat normal food, like you see people eating on sit-coms. Not like what we eat, which is pizza or toast or whatever we dial out of the phone book. His mum and dad take turns and cook. Healthy food. Chicken and vegetables and rice and whatever. Take turns talking about every trivial thing that they thought about during the day. Jokes. They tease each other.

Is has three sisters. They're all pretty okay. Yeah. But they're younger than me, so it doesn't count. It would be creepy to hook up with your friend's sister, anyway, right? The oldest one is Stasia and she's ... well, she's ... I like her. But she's only fifteen. Maybe she's sixteen now. I don't know. I don't talk to her much because I'd probably sound like all the other jerks who are always *talking* to her.

Israel has a tattoo of a blue and green snake that curls around his whole leg. His dad did that. He's an artist. He said all the kids could have one piece, just one, and they better choose carefully. Israel's is cool but I wouldn't have picked it. It's corny, too.

It's obvious.

I want to know where Stasia's is. Or if she has one. One of the other girls — is it Annie or Dee? — has a frog on her shoulder. Like a cartoon.

She'll probably want to get that removed one day.

I've never seen Stasia's, so if it's there, it must be some-where hidden. Somewhere that I can't see. I wish I could.

No, I shouldn't think of her that way. I'm a creep. She's like a sister to me.

I have a lot of friends. Friends who are girls. Friends who are boys. Whatever. There's a girl, Michael (yeah, I know, it's a guy's name) who has crushed on me for years. It's creepy but it's also flattering. It's like everyone knows about it and so it's just there. It is what it is. I guess I've kind of just accepted that she'll probably be my girlfriend sooner or later.

I just don't feel like I really want a girlfriend right now. I guess I do. Who doesn't want a girlfriend?

Weirdos, that's who. Losers. I'm not a loser. Ask anyone. People like me. I don't know why. I guess they don't have a reason not to. I try to be nice to people. I try to think about their feelings.

After Joe died, I saw a therapist for a couple of months. We talked about feelings a lot. He said I was very empathetic. I guess he must be right. He's the expert.

To tell you the truth, sometimes I just want to be alone. Not that I ever really am, but aren't we all alone? I guess that's philosophy or some shit like Joe would have liked. I'm interested in it, but not like he was. I won't throw everything away for some alternate reality. I won't let it make me crazy.

A lot of my friends are psyched for college for the partying. I guess I could care about that, but I don't. Spring break? Whatever. I mean, I'm a guy, so sure, I'm happy to look at drunk girls in bikinis. Why not? But I wouldn't want to get with them. I wouldn't want to be out of control myself.

I think I'd like to study everything that I think is interesting. Archaeology would be okay. I don't know. Architecture. I'd rather study than get wasted and sleep in my own puke. I'd rather feel like I was accomplishing something. Like I was getting something back instead of just a headache and a blacked-out memory.

I'm just not gonna get excited about drinking so much that I shake the next day. I just don't want it. I wonder if there's such a thing as a college where that doesn't go down. Where people read books and talk about stuff and where they're really interested in things other than themselves. Where rowing is important.

Can schools like that make you smart? Or are they just using kids up for their athleticism and then letting them vanish into the world, just as dumb as when they arrived?

And, after all, is any of it what I want? What the fuck do I want? What do I want for forever?

Rowing?

I like other stuff, too. I'm not okay to do just one thing, that's the problem. I'd never admit it, but I like biology. But I never study enough and it always seems like I'm not sure what we're doing, like I'm always about a month behind. Man, I hope I pass this test. I can't fail again, Mr. Morgenthal told me. He's gonna flunk me out. He hates athletes, I know it. He's a little guy, and round. The little round guys always pick on us. They do.

I've got to pass. I just do.

Then, after school, the baskets. That's what I'll do. I quickly text Is to see if he wants to come and do some one-on-one with me but just as quickly he answers, no can do, dude. It doesn't matter. I wanted to be alone, anyway. Just me and the bum and the basketball. That's all.

Michael

3

"*Come on,*" *says* Chelsea. "A little to the left."

"Left of what?" says Angene. "*You* do it. I don't know what you mean."

"Get Michael to do it," says Chelsea. "She knows. *Left.* How hard is that?" Chelsea can't move because if she does the raccoon will fall off her newly shaved (and slippery) head. She's wearing nothing but some kind of made-from-tree-leaves bikini and body paint. She's standing on a cable suspended between two chairs that are bolted to the floor, and the raccoon is teetering dangerously.

"I'm busy," says Michael. She rolls a glass marble from a dish full of them toward her brother, Sully. He appreciates marbles. The glass, the colours, the refractions they make. It looks like he does, anyway. He picks it up, holds it up to the light. She's not sure, but she could swear that he almost smiles. Poor perfect Sully. So beautiful, but he's not really there, not in the way that most people are. His own mind is a universe that he rarely steps out of. Chelsea jumps down off the cable with a thud, the raccoon falling to the floor. She comes over and grabs another marble from the dish on the table and starts tossing it up and down. It sparkles yellow-green in the light. Sully flinches.

"This shot just isn't working," says Chelsea. "I don't know. It's not right."

"You can say that again," mutters Michael, under her breath. She grabs the marble and gives it to Sully, who visibly relaxes, rolling it around in his palm. The bright spotlights make his hair look exactly like metallic gold thread, a look that Michael herself has her hairdresser emulate for about four hundred dollars a month. But on Sully, it's natural. It's incredible. She fights an urge to touch it. Sully doesn't much like being touched.

Chelsea slumps down next to Michael at the table. Michael can smell her sister's freshly shaved head; it smells like men's shaving lotion. Disgusting.

"Your head stinks," she says.

Chelsea glares, pushes back the chair, goes back to the shot. Repositions herself with a lot of shouting and swearing. Michael wills herself not to look up, but she can't help it. She looks up. Chelsea's body is almost perfect, but she has cellulite on her legs that is making Michael anxious. "Do some leg lifts!" she wants to shout. "Go for a run!"

Her other sister, Angene (fully clothed, armed with a giant, expensive-looking camera) is trying to wrestle three huge stuffed wolves into position to make them look like they are attacking Chelsea. Angene is the quieter of the two. She works away in the background while Chelsea growls and poses. Angene is fat. Chelsea is mostly thin. Angene is almost all hair. Chelsea is bald. Opposites, yet something about them is so alike. More than just the flapping flesh on their upper arms. More than their identical voices. You can tell they are sisters, just at a glance.

"You guys are seriously disturbed," Michael says. "It's like a freak show in here. This can't be good for Sully."

"It's *art*," says Chelsea. "He likes it, don't you, Sully? When will you understand, Mike? You have to learn to stretch yourself."

"Okay. Like, maybe, never," says Michael. "I'm not helping."

"Please?" says Angene. "C'mon, little sis. I don't know if I can do this by myself, I need someone to hold this beast. It's too windy to balance him." Angene's hair is blowing into her mouth and sticking to her lip gloss. For some reason, a fan is on full blast. Why does there need to be a fan? It's already too cold in the room. Like a morgue, Michael thinks. Like a walk-in fridge. She hates to be cold, more than anything. Being cold, freezing to death, that's the worst thing she can imagine. Sully seems unaffected by it, but still, he must be chilled.

He's sitting up straight in his special chair. It's not a wheelchair or anything like that; he's not physically disabled. Not really. He just sometimes needs help to move or dress, but it's less out of a need for actual help and more because he doesn't seem to be able to think of how to do it or why. Secretly Michael believes it's because he's thinking things that are so much more important. Thinking things that aren't so mundane as how to do up a zipper or have a conversation. Deep things. His chair is a wooden chair that he loves, or seems to love. He won't sit on anything else.

Sully is autistic. Not just mildly autistic, or Asperger's. Einstein had that, people say. It's almost trendy right now, in the news all the time. Sully's not like that, he's full-on autistic ("low-functioning," they call it, but she hates that phrase), plus some other stuff that Michael can't remember the labels for. He doesn't talk. Mostly he just sits. He looks at things. He thinks. He has the most perfectly smooth skin. He's model-beautiful, picture perfect. The crescent-shaped cheekbones slung high under his gold-flecked eyes.

"No," says Michael, pulling a hunk of flawlessly trimmed blonde hair in front of her eyes to inspect it for split ends. "I don't want your total creepy weirdness rubbing off on me."

"It wouldn't hurt you to be more creative. It would help open you up," says Chelsea. She coughs. Again. She's off-balance. She wobbles. Topples off the cable with a crash. "Damn it!" There is a series of thuds as the raccoon bounces along the floor and over to where Michael is sitting at the only table in the whole enormous, mostly empty living room-cum-photo studio. The stuffed dead raccoon stares up at her with its repulsive glass eyes. The eyes remind her of Yale and her one scary, unblinking blue eye. She had a bad dream just last night where Yale stared at her hard with that eye and smoke started curling up from the flesh on her arm.

The dream made her sweat. She hates sweating. Uncomfortable. Sticky.

Smelly.

Human.

She nudges the raccoon hard with her foot and it rocks over onto its back, sliding back toward her sisters on the highly waxed floor. It's ridiculous. It's like a funhouse. *No one lives like this*, she thinks.

No one should have to. It's too weird to be real. Too weird to be *her* reality, anyway.

"Disgusting," she says. "Did you give Sully any food before I got home?" Sully likes chocolate cookies. Bananas. Chocolate milk. But he can't ask for it and her stupid sisters get so caught up in their "art," they sometimes forget to ask.

"No," says Angene. "I'll get him something in a sec."

"I'll do it," says Michael. "Don't knock yourself out." She stomps to the kitchen and makes the snack, takes it out and puts it on his lap. He doesn't acknowledge her, doesn't look her in the eye, but he does start eating like he's starving. She touches his head. She can't help it. He doesn't pull away, but she can feel him tighten.

"Sorry," she whispers. She never really knows how to take him. Honestly, he sometimes scares her. His *absence*.

She grabs her books and heads for the stairs. Homework can wait. Who cares? It's not like knowing how to calculate how fast her car has to go to get away from a train coming in the opposite direction if x equals blah, blah, blah, is ever going to matter to her. "Freaks," she mutters over her shoulder in the direction of her sisters. "Not you, Sully," she adds. "But definitely *you*," she says to the stuffed squirrel frozen in mid-scramble halfway up the railing.

She's *never* been able to stand the dead animals. It didn't matter how much her parents tried to make them into toys, tried to convince her they were "cute," they still gave her (still *give* her, in fact) bad dreams.

In her room (a Dead-Animal-Free Zone), she plonks herself down on the thick white throw rug and does sit-ups until she feels sick. Picks the carpet fluff off her pants.

Inspects herself in the floor-to-ceiling mirror for pimples, ripples, flaws. Admires her rib bones. She's *almost* perfectly skinny. Close enough that she can almost see it. She's skinny enough that her head looks just a bit too big. Perfectly balanced in its imbalance. Like a lollipop girl, those thin girls in magazines. Big head, big eyes, insect-like body that barely exists floating somewhere underneath.

Not finding any big flaw to focus on, she settles on trimming the tiny hairs on her eyebrows so that they are exactly, precisely symmetrical. She plucks out each one of the nearly invisible hairs from her top lip, which hurts. Makes her eyes water. Makes her sneeze.

"Suffer to be beautiful," she reminds herself. Her grandmother (Granny Aggie, not Grandma Jane) was a fashion model in the 1950s. She's the one who named Michael. She practically raised her, really. For a while, Michael couldn't stand to be in her parents' house. It was mostly the dead animals but also her sisters and the way they used up all her parents' attention. And Sully hasn't always been so easy. Not that he's actually easy now, but at least he's calm.

Granny Aggie had let her stay for a week or two or three each month. She was the only one who ever really listened to Michael. She's the only one who made Michael feel like she could do anything she wanted to do. That she was special. She let Michael wear her clothes and didn't make her feel like an annoying kid. She took her seriously, or made her feel that way. And she *got* it; she understood that looking good was important. She understood why.

And then, one day, she died. Not in front of Michael, thank God. Michael couldn't have handled it. She just bent over to tie her shoe, and bam, she was gone. She left a ton of money to Michael, and to Michael's parents. Enough that Michael can have whatever she wants, whenever she wants it. She'd rather have Granny Aggie back; she'd rather have an adult to talk to about her life. To help her figure it all out. But the money is nice, too. Buys her lots of expensive jeans. Nice car. Expensive haircuts. Good teeth. Her teeth aren't even real; they're veneers, just like all the movie stars have. Granny gave them to her for her fifteenth birthday when it seemed like her teeth were going to need braces. Veneers were a better, prettier choice. Granny Aggie wouldn't have wanted Michael to have a mouth full of plastic and elastics. No way.

She gave Michael a lot of advice. Taught her a lot of important things, mostly about being pretty. Always being pretty. Never, ever letting anyone see you looking less than your best. She also gave Michael a lot of clothes, which are sadly too mothballed to wear, but cool in a vintage actress-at-the-Oscars kind of glamorama way.

Grandma Jane never gave her anything but a cigarette-smoke headache. Michael wrinkles her nose in disgust at the memory. Fat old Grandma Jane and her funny-tasting cookies and rum in coffee mugs.

Both of them are gone, Grandma Jane not actually dead but stinking it up in some old age home, not knowing who anyone is, soiling herself. Teeth in a glass by her bed. Visiting her is a nightmare. Michael would rather tie her shoe and drop dead than ever be the slobbery unkempt mess that is Grandma Jane.

She sighs. She misses Granny Aggie, probably the only semi-normal, semi-gorgeous, semi-cool person in her whole family tree. Misses her so much she's sure she can actually feel the pain of it in her chest. A zing of sorrow.

Michael flosses her teeth, applies a facial mask. She moves the rug off the floor and sits down on the hardwood. Closes her eyes and crosses her legs. Concentrates on her breathing. Her bony butt hurts from sitting there, but she sticks with it. Actually, she likes that it hurts. Likes that she's aware of her bones on the hard floor. It feels good. It feels like she's won.

Meditation is her new "thing." She even got some new cute meditation clothes to celebrate her adventure into being "spiritual." Yoga pants, tanks that breathe and wick away sweat, darling shoes that are almost like ballet slippers (pink, too) designed by a famous musician's daughter.

She thinks about her clothes breathing, imagines them moving.

Creepy.

Focus, she thinks. *In out in out inoutinoutinoutinout.*

Her head spins a bit, so she lies on her back. Stares at the ceiling. Holds her breath. Plugs her nose. Will that fix it? She rolls over and presses her forehead into the cool wood.

There.

Her therapist, whose name is Hope (Is that made up? Michael wonders) suggested that she try meditation every day. An hour to just *breathe*. She is theoretically treating Michael for night terrors (which Michael wants to explain would probably go away if the dead animals were to vanish from her house), but they have never actually talked about the dreams themselves.

Lame. Not that she really wants to talk about them; they sound so stupid when she says anything about them out loud. Dead stuffed animal zombies. Sounds like a dumb movie more than anything else. One too silly to be really scary.

Hope is okay. The most important factor in her relationship with Hope is that Hope is also her mother's best friend, which completely prevents Michael from talking to her about anything real. The bad dreams are the least of Michael's problems. If she told Hope something truly bad, like how she feels worthless sometimes; like how she sometimes envies Sully who never has to perform, never has to do anything; how she feels like an alien in her family and a fake everywhere else, faker than her fake "friends" who — if she's being honest — are the embodiment of everything she's afraid that she is herself. How Michael hates herself if she spots a flaw in the mirror — like really, really hates herself. *Loathes*. But if she admitted all that, Hope would no doubt tell on her. And her mother *worrying* about her is worse than her mother ignoring her, as she usually does, since she's busy stuffing dead animals from around the world and posing them for creepy photographs and calendars and greeting cards. Family pets, posed to look like they're sleeping. Hunting trophies posed to look like they want to escape. Roadkill rebuilt to resemble its former self. The most sick and twisted family business she could ever imagine, much less participate in.

And with all Granny Aggie's money, they don't even *have* to do it. They do it because they like it. They love it. They think it's *art*. Why they can't just slap some paint on a canvas instead, Michael has no idea. There's art, and then there's just, well, a horror show. This is definitely the latter.

She shudders.

Michael doesn't usually follow Hope's suggestions (nettle tea, Chinese herbs, fasting, support groups), but this meditation sounded okay. Not too kooky. The problem is that sitting doing nothing makes her think about too much stuff. Like Tony, her not-yet-but-soon-to-be-boyfriend. First she thinks about what she said to him at lunch, which was so embarrassing she blushes again now.

She said, "You're so welcome, Tone."

That's all.

It doesn't *sound* embarrassing taken out of context, but it turned out he hadn't said thank you. Well, not to her. He was talking to someone else, not anything to do with her. She'd just blurted. She was nervous. He was so close. And it was so loud, her own voice. Gross. And "Tone"? What was up with that?

She's an idiot.

He had given her that look. That particular look of his that said, "You're not worth my time."

Michael can't stand to be not wanted. It makes her want to hurt herself in some fundamental — but non-marking — way.

She tries hard to think about something other than Tony. About the way he handed Madison her pompoms when she dropped them on the way into the gym. (All the girls from the gymnastics team also cheer, except Yale, of course, who tried out but didn't make the team. "Not the right *look*," the coach said. "She'd put the balance off." And Michael, feeling like what that meant was "not pretty enough," agreed even though she felt funny about it.)

Tony. She thinks about the way he got flustered in math and she just wanted to help him, give him the answer, rescue him from his own, well, inherent dumbness. But he *is* dumb. Like a golden retriever or something. Dumb but lovable. Dumb but still valuable somehow, still worth talking to, still interesting.

And so what? What's wrong with being dumb? It's just like he's simpler than most people. Wouldn't talk her ear off about idealistic crap like saving the world or curing cancer or all the other pretentious bullshit she's noticed that the kids in her class are tending toward as graduation approaches. Overly dramatic, almost fake "smarts." Stuff they don't know anything about, but pretend to know so they look informed.

Besides which, Tony's so hot. Much hotter than he could know. Those *eyes*. His eyelashes — black, long. Close up, they look like feathers. Surreal. And his body. Well, everyone knows that rowers have the best bodies. Totally cut abs. Crazy fine muscles that look like they're sculpted out of stone.

In the back of her mind, Michael has an idea that if she and Tony someday were to get married, have a baby, it would be so gorgeous. Her fairness combined with his darkness would be perfect.

Not that she's thinking about marrying him. So limiting to marry your high school boyfriend (not that he is, but he *will* be). So naïve to limit your options. She's sure that ultimately there is something bigger and better out there for her. Someone like Justin Timberlake. Someone like George Clooney, but younger. Someone, well, famous. Someone who can take her away from the life she has now, from this house, from her family.

Still. It's hard to imagine a boy better looking than Tony. He's *so* much more beautiful than that obnoxious

Israel, who walks around the school like he owns it. She can tell that Tony doesn't know how awful Israel is, how arrogant. Tony has no arrogance. He looks like he feels uncomfortable in himself. She can relate. She will *not* think about the way she saw him looking at Stasia Santiago when he thought no one was watching. He was staring. *Ogling*. Were they together?

Not possible. No, Stasia is just Israel's sister. There wouldn't be anything there.

Or would there?

Her heartbeat speeds up and she opens her eyes. Meditation sucks, she thinks. She should call someone. Aurelia, or one of the other Girls. Anyone to distract her. Aurelia is such a vicious bitchy girl; she always somehow makes Michael feel better. It's something to do with the way that Aurie slams everyone else, what everyone is wearing, how they look and act, what they say. Like she's the judge and jury and no one else's opinion matters. It's mean, but because Michael knows she's exempt from it, she's also safe. It doesn't make sense, but it's true. And Aurelia always has something new to say, that's for sure. Probably has some bitchy gossip about Stasia that would cheer Michael up at the same time as making her feel guilty for being happy about it.

Stasia has black hair that she wears loose down her back. For a second, Michael wishes so hard that her own hair was dark that she can almost feel it changing. She wishes she looked exotic. She's too pale to be exotic. It isn't fair. Even with a tan, she ends up looking like a cheap Malibu Barbie and not like a mysterious foreign beauty.

She stretches. Her cramps are killing her. Thinking about cramps makes her think about poor ridiculous Yale getting her period in front of everyone. Was it, like, her *first* period? At seventeen? Doesn't she have a clue?

There is something about that girl that is just so hope less. Michael frowns. Hopeless. She wishes she didn't care, that she could just write her off like the other girls have, but she does care. She can't not care. She wants to somehow give her some advice. Do something to help her. To save her from herself. Stop her from embarrassing herself any further. *Normalize* her. Tell her, for example, that all the fake tattoos are too much. Show her how to put on her makeup so she doesn't look like either a goth freak or a kid who stole Mummy's mascara.

She gets up and goes into her own bathroom (no dead animals there either) and scrubs her face clean. Her skin looks ideal. She nods, satisfied, trims one hair in her bangs that looks slightly longer than the others. For no reason (she's not going out, no one to impress), she plugs in the straightening iron and starts the process of perfecting her hair. She has to look as good as she can. That's the whole thing. If she doesn't look just so, she can't breathe. Meditation or no meditation.

What she really needs, she thinks, is medication. Not meditation. Some nice little pill. Something to make her feel as relaxed and happy as she always tries to appear. She's heard stories; she knows such a pill exists. All those famous It girls take them, sometimes too much (and end up in rehab). She should, too. She's an It girl. Sort of. Well, within the confines of her high school she is. But her parents would never give her the okay. Hope doesn't even believe in Prozac. Hope believes in self. Hope believes in mind power. Hope believes in St. John's wort. And, Michael happens to know, Hope drinks a lot of wine.

It's not fair. Sully takes pills. He takes Risperdal and Prozac. Without those pills, he acts out more. Suddenly flips out. Gets mad super easily. With them, he's calm. She could swipe some of his maybe, but no. She'd never do that. Sully is sacred. She'd never take anything from him. Never.

Maybe she can buy something on the internet, Michael thinks. She wouldn't specifically know what to get though. Ritalin? Prozac? Xanax? Probably not a good idea to experiment. She knows all the names but isn't that sure which pill does what or why. Or how. That Nicole Richie was in treatment for heroin addiction, but heroin sounds too deadly. Too crazy, too dangerous, too scary, even for her.

She likes to think that she's brave, but really she knows it's not true. Most things scare her. Drugs. Sex. Life in general.

She squints as she concentrates on smoothing her hair. The smell of the hot iron makes her feel better. Tomorrow she won't say anything stupid to Tony. Tomorrow she will think of some way to get him to like her. Something. It's not like he *doesn't* like her; he's just so nice, he likes everyone. And so everyone likes him.

Michael isn't stupid. She knows lots of people don't like her. Because she's pretty. And she hates that they hate her — hates herself, anyway, more than they could. Maybe if she was nicer overall, she thinks. Maybe if she, like Tony, was just nice to everyone, then everyone would like her back. Like Yale, for example. It wouldn't kill her to be nice to Yale. Especially now that everyone hates her so much for the whole gymnastics incident. She can be a better person — she *is* a better person — than all the girls who are still snickering when Yale walks by, still making dumb jokes, still sticking Kotex pads on her locker, still hating on the girl.

And it's hardly like she chose it, right? It was an accident, one that could happen to anyone. Well, any girl, at least. But no one has her back about it. It must suck to be completely socially outcast. Michael wouldn't know: she's always had lots of friends, girls she knows would trade places with her in a second, even if her life includes having to look at a thousand stuffed dead animals every day on her way to the kitchen to make her dry wheat toast. She's pretty. She's smart. She's a good athlete. Who wouldn't want to be her?

I mean, really, Michael thinks. *What would Granny Aggie do?*

She'd be nice, that's what. In spite of everything, even though she looked like she could be a totally snobby bitch, Granny Aggie was always nice.

Michael would never accidentally get her period, though, so she can't relate. Not to that. She gets the cramps a day before. The pain that doubles her over. She'd never be caught off-guard. In a way, she's both jealous and mystified. Imagine a life where you didn't know when your period would start. When your body didn't freak out the second the egg dropped, or whatever.

She can't stop thinking of Tony staring at Stasia, bouncing his stupid basketball with one hand. The image is like a song stuck in her head that she can't get out. Israel trying to get his attention, clowning. A couple of girls, friends of Stasia's, younger girls — so Michael obviously doesn't know their names — noticing Tony noticing Stasia.

Everywhere Tony goes, there seem to be lots of other people. Always Israel. Usually girls. A lump forms in her throat. Why isn't she good enough?

She blames everything. Maybe she's *too* pretty. Maybe she's *too* smart. She should act dumber. Maybe it's the fact that she lives in a weird house. Maybe it's the stupid business that her parents run. A horror movie joke.

For years, she told people her parents were animal doctors. Not exactly true, but sort of. And then Israel's dumb, ugly dog got hit by a car in the next block and he had come running up the driveway, the stinky broken dog in his arms, panicking, and her dad had told the truth: not an animal doctor, an animal *stuffer*. Taxidermy, he explained. He still helped (well, the dog died, anyway), but after that everyone knew. For about a week, she knew people were whispering about her.

"Ugh," she says out loud.

It was the worst week of her life.

She makes some final adjustments in the bathroom mirror. Smears on her expensive moisturizer (she read in *InStyle* that Courtney Cox uses it, and she has the best skin). Her hair shimmers. *It's okay*, she thinks. *I look okay*. She goes into her room to pick out her clothes for the next day. She can't sleep unless everything is laid out perfectly, two outfits so she can choose in the morning depending on the weather. She opens her closet and a marmot falls out.

She screams.

"Freaks!" she yells, throwing the marmot down the stairs.

"Mike," yells her mum. "Don't throw the merchandise!"

"Whatever," Michael says. "Don't put the disgusting merchandise in my closet!"

"Chelsea! Angene!" she hears her mother yell. "Angene!" Then louder, "CHELSEA! ANGENE! NOW!"

She closes the door, satisfied that her sisters will be in trouble again. Not that they care. It doesn't matter as much for them. They're both over twenty-one. They can come and go as they please. They aren't stuck here in this funhouse of glass eyes and fur, waiting for the day they can escape. Of course, *why* they are still here is a mystery.

Michael goes to her closet. *Blue*, she thinks. She feels like wearing blue. It brings out her eyes. After she's done that, she'll go down and eat her dark green leafy salad and exactly three ounces of chicken. An apple. Two glasses of water to get to her eight for the day.

The phone beeps out her favourite song. She drops her pale blue cashmere cardigan and races to find it. Where is it? In a drawer? In the pocket of her jacket? She almost screams. After all, it might be someone important. Maybe this time, it's Tony.

Maybe.

Yale

4

This thing — this *gift*, if that's what it is (am I supposed to know how to use it or was it just a one-time thing?) — is freaking me out. I can't think about much else. Even though I haven't vanished again, not yet, everything is different.

For one thing, I can see things better. Not just *better*, but ridiculously well. My vision is so good that its intensity is becoming overwhelming; sudden flashes of light — even the TV — make me feel faint. I can see things, details that don't even exist. Like every atom or molecule or cell. I can see colours that I've never seen, in-between colours that are almost just light. I can see the movement of dust mites on the surface of the carpet.

I can see too much.

Like I can see the lines around my mum's eyes, but deeper than that. The redness hiding in the bottom of the lines, under a nearly invisible sheen of oil. The filmy pot haze that lurks over my dad's pupils. The hair follicles of his shaved beard. Tiny flecks of dried skin that cling to the edge of his nostrils.

I feel like I can see *inside* them.

What else does it mean? What am I supposed to be seeing that I couldn't see before? Is it about me? Or something bigger than me?

And who can I ask?

I don't know. But I know it's going to change my life. It already has. It's like power in a way that I can't pinpoint, but somehow I feel better. In control.

Not in a Michael-way, but in a completely different way. In a strong way.

I'm excited. But also I'm scared.

I've never been so aware of all my parts. I know that sounds ridiculous, but it's true. I've never felt my fingers moving. Obviously I know they move, but I've never been so aware of it. Every tendon, every muscle, every breath, every heartbeat. My mouth feels like it is full of cheese that's too thick to chew, but it's just air and saliva. My eyelashes tickle my cheeks. I swear, I can feel my hair growing. When I take a drag of my clove cigarette, the flavour feels like it's popping out of every pore of my skin, saturating me with spice.

My hands shake and shake. If you thought I was jittery before, well, now it's a whole new game. Now I feel electrocuted. I feel currents coursing through me that can't exist. Like lightning struck or is still striking.

I'm ignited.

But what am I supposed to do with it?

I have *no* idea.

It feels like it has to have a purpose, a reason. Like a calling, but more than that and not necessarily something to do with God, if God, in fact, exists.

I do what I always do. I'm trying to be normal, but really I'm just holding my breath, waiting for it to happen again. Waiting for someone to tell me what's happening. Waiting to figure out what to do.

I go to practice. As I ride to school on my scooter, I feel like the vibration might propel me into space. The exhaust is as thick as soup, spiralling behind me like spilled paint. The blueness of the sky is so sharp it almost hurts. The birds create such a cacophony, I almost want to plug my ears. Everything is a thousand times what it was before. A million.

I make it to school on time, early even. Get to the gym first. I'm alone in there except for Coach, who is setting up equipment with Mr. Hastlewaite, the math teacher.

It takes forever. I do sit-ups while I wait. Push-ups. Stretches. Everything feels like more than it should. I'm so wired. I want to lift some heavy weights or something. Do something to feel anchored down.

Then, finally, The Girls tumble in. Their shoes squeaking and thudding. Giggling about something, as always. Michael's hair in twin ponytails, that on anyone else would make them look two years old. Looking perfect. Relaxed. Happy. She gives me a half-smile while the other girls seem to look right through me, as though I don't exist. I get that: they've written me off.

Fine.

Whatever.

I knew they would act like this. After all, they saw and didn't tell me. They let me keep going, let everyone see, practically held me up so the school could laugh.

I committed the worst sin of all, didn't I? I *embarrassed* myself. Unforgivable.

I'm on the beam, trying to fake normalcy, trying to pretend to be me instead of whatever I'm becoming. Trying to focus on nothing but the wood under my feet and hands, the solid thunk of my body moving away from the beam in a jump or a twist and then back onto it. Trying to ignore the sweat-soaked aura of everything, the harsh flicker in the bank of fluorescent lights, the swirling movement of the wood, which can't be moving but seems like it is, and the smattering of sharp glances I keep getting from my so-called teammates.

Other than the occasional whispers between them, it's pretty quiet in the gym except for the sound of Michael talking to herself as she practises her floor routine. It's all thud, thud, thud, whisper, whisper. She always does this and I can never hear what she says, but today I can.

She's saying, "Not good enough, not good enough, loser, loser, loser. Fuck. Shit. Damn. Do it again. Again, again."

I try not to watch her, but I can't help it. It's not that she's good or bad or indifferent, it's just that she's compelling to see. She makes you watch. I force myself to look away, to stare at the grains of varnished wood of the beam. I tell myself it's solid, not moving. But it is. Every nuance of colour. It's crazy, is what it is. For a second I feel dizzy, and then I force myself to move, to try to do my round-off dismount that Coach is waiting to see.

And I miss.

Completely.

At first it's more of a sound than a feeling, like I hear the smack of my head against the wood like a hammer on a nail. It echoes and echoes. How could it sound so metallic? Bone on wood, nothing tin.

I realize, *Oh, my head.*

Aurelia and Madison are beside me in a flash. I flinch, like I'm worried they might kick me. You never know. They had been close, waiting for their turn to talk to Coach, who seems now to have vanished — where did she go? Shouldn't she be helping me?

While they waited, they'd been staring and whispering to each other about what I would have once guessed was *me*, but now I know was just some crap about a girl named Marnie Sims who graduated last year and apparently slept with Israel Santiago and then had to have an abortion.

Who cares?

Is it true?

"You're bleeding!" shrieks Aurelia, which completely pierces my brain, like an arrow.

"Oh my God," Madison says. "COACH! COACH!" Which also doesn't help, her words ringing like church bells, too loud. Coach is there after all, there already, struck mute somehow. She seems helpless, like it hasn't occurred to her that she might be called upon in this kind of emergency. Ever.

"Too loud," I whisper. "Can you get me a towel or something? Some ice?"

I squint up at them from where I'm lying on the vinyl crash pad, the plastic smell of it making me queasy, blood trickling down my cheek and I swear I can feel it moving, feel every bit of it making a rivulet on my cheek, feel my cheek where it's touching, feel my brain ricocheting from the blow, feel it all.

I feel too much. I don't like it. I want it to stop. This time, for real. What felt, for twenty-four hours, like an adventure now feels like something sinister. Scary.

My hands are shaking so hard, all the way up my arms. Oh, it's all of me. I'm shaking. Coach says, "Don't move!" Like this is good and worthwhile advice. I move off the crash pad and onto the hardwood, it seems safer that way and less smelly. More solid. It slows the shaking.

"I mean it!" she adds, as if it isn't too late.

Then Michael is there; she looks at me and shudders so hard I can feel it through the floor. "Blood," she says, and keels over in a dead faint (or a fake faint) and then the attention is gone from me, all of them crowded around her while I lie there, invisible. But not *actually*. I'm here, I feel like shouting, only the shouting would hurt my head, my ears, my being.

Finally, there's an icepack (too cold), bandages (too tight), Coach shining a light (too bright) into my eyes and declaring that I'm okay. Her breath is heavy with onions and garlic and it's half past seven in the morning. How is that possible?

Disgusting.

I hear Aurelia whisper to Sam, "She sure bleeds a lot." Both of them snickering. Oh, that's funny. Why do I care so much what they think? Tears sting my eyes. Bleeding, bleeding. So hilarious.

I feel so strange. Light-headed. Faint.

Which all sets me up for a long, horrible day. I won't bore you with the details of the long, horrible classes. My throbbing headache. The feeling that I'm not really quite here. But it's worse than that. There's more: like I wasn't already the punchline to every giggle in the hallway, now I'm stuck with a bandage on my head that *looks* like a maxi-pad.

"I think you're wearing that in the wrong place, girl," someone shouts. Is it Matti? I can't tell. Probably I deserved it, from him. After all, I did puke on his lap. That was humiliating, too. And pretty unforgivable, I guess, from his perspective. I wonder why the embarrassment of *that* didn't make me disappear. I just passed out. Barf in my hair. On the ground.

I'm gross.

No wonder everyone hates me.

I will myself to vanish, but it doesn't work. I crave it. I want it. I want to be able to do it at will. I mean, why not? But nothing works.

The jokes go on and on. The whispers, all of which I can hear. I don't want to hear them. I stick my iPod earphones in and blast the music when I'm in the hall, but I can still tell people are looking and laughing. Only Anika shoots me a sympathetic look, and I'm so grateful I nearly cry.

The day takes forever. Forever and ever.

As soon as the last bell goes, I run. Trip on the stairs and stumble, knocking over some smaller kid with an armful of books. "Sorry," I shout over my shoulder but I can't stop to help him. I have to get out of there.

I walk home. I feel like I could run the whole way. I feel like I could walk forever. I find a scrap of paper in my backpack, a pen. I write down, "Too strong." It seems important to write it down somehow. Like otherwise, I might forget this feeling, this passing second.

I feel like if I passed a car accident or something, someone trapped under a vehicle, I could lift it off with my pinkie. I want to lift a car off someone.

I write the word "superhero," followed by a question mark. Feeling stupid, I stuff the scrap of paper into my jeans pocket.

I run a few blocks, my bag slamming into my back, but it doesn't make me feel any different. Doesn't take away the feeling.

My parents are in the kitchen when I get home. Eating Alphagetti straight from the can. Sharing a spoon. I eye them suspiciously. Maybe they *know*. They're somehow in on it, like ... But no, that can't be true. They can hardly be experimenting mad scientists. They're like *children*.

"How's your world?" Dad says.

I hesitate for a minute. Like I'm going to tell them. "Okay," I say. "Good enough."

"What's wrong?" he says.

"Nothing," I say. "Nothing is wrong. I'm hungry. Is there anything other than that crap to eat?"

"It's not crap," says Mum. "It's good."

"I've got to go to my room," I say.

"Something's wrong," says Dad. "I sense it with my dad-sense."

"Dad," I say. "Please don't be weird. I've had enough weird for the day." I drop my bag on the floor. Chuck my jacket on the back of a chair. My arms are tingling.

"You should talk to us," says Dad. "Tell us about your day. We're interested."

"Yeah," I say. "Sure. Only nothing happened."

"Nothing?" says Mum. "What's that on your head?"

"My head?" I'd forgotten. I reach up and touch the bandage. Under it, a shot of pain zings down my forehead through my cheek to my tooth. "Oh. That. Well, I fell."

"I fell," mimics Dad. "That's a lot of information, thanks."

"I fell off the beam," I say. "The balance beam. I fell on my head. What more do you need to know?" It's stupid, but I'm mad at him for asking. I'm mad at him when he doesn't ask about my day, mad when he does. He has Alphagetti sauce dripping down his chin. His T-shirt features The Clash. He takes a huge gulp of milk right from the container.

"Looks painful," he says.

"Yeah," I say. "It sucks."

Out of nowhere, my mum says, "I understand more of what you are going through than you think. I was a teenager myself once, you know." She bites into an apple to punctuate this. I can see a spray of juice at impact, glistening in the light.

"We were teenagers," Dad echoes. "Yes."

"You still are," I say meanly. But they take it as a compliment.

"Thanks, honey," says Mum. "I feel old today."

"Huh," I say. I take off my shoes. And socks. The lino is crumb-covered underfoot. Gross. Like stepping on a million tiny pebbles. I make my way to the fridge and peer in, a blast of cold stinging my eyes when I open the door. A brownish array of celery and a few limp carrots. Some uncooked ground beef. A half-dozen eggs. I put the eggs on the counter and start making an omelette.

My dad sighs. "It's hard to be a teenager," he says.

"I guess," I say. "It's probably not as hard as being an adult, say. Having to earn a living. Be a grown-up." I say it pointedly. But he doesn't get the implication. The frying pan is filthy. I put it in the sink and start scrubbing.

"Once I jumped off a bridge," says Dad. "Just to test, you know? What would happen?"

"Dad," I say. "Please. I'm not in the mood for one of your stories."

"I was drunk," he says. "Don't ever drink, honey. It messes you up."

"Totally unlike the drugs you smoke," I say.

"Yeah," he says. "It's different. That's natural."

"Huh," is all I say. And even that is an effort. Suddenly I'm so tired. Cracking the eggs seems like a lot of trouble. If this is some kind of science experiment that I'm unwittingly participating in, it's a pretty weird one. Take two half-baked parents and one invisible child, and what do you get?

I leave the eggs bubbling in the pan, dig the scrap of paper out of my pocket and write, "Definitely not an experiment."

I see them look at each other with a look that says, "She's in trouble! We must help! And yet we should go back downstairs and pretend everything is normal!"

So they go.

It's easier, after all. I don't blame them. I wish I had somewhere to go to get away from me, too.

"I just have a headache," I tell them, even though they aren't there to hear. I dump the omelette out onto a plate. It tastes really good. Incredibly good. It's so good I have to close my eyes to eat it.

Then just like that, a bird flies into the glass. *Wham.* The thud almost knocks me sideways, my heart racing in my throat like crazy, the glass trembling in a vibrato. So loud.

I try to calm down. Breathe. I feel like I need to try to think. What is happening to me?

The first day after, I figured that everyone knew. About the *disappearing*, not about my period. I was surprised that they didn't but also not surprised. A lot of people were at the meet. Gymnastics is popular. Boys like to think about the girls all twisted up, probably naked. Girls like to envy.

So many people saw. Or didn't see.

But nobody saw. Or nobody said, maybe they thought they'd all imagined it. The vanishing, that is. They all saw the blood. They all talked about *that*. Ha, ha. So, *so* funny. Ha dee ha.

Assholes.

Like getting my period (which probably every girl in the school, except the anorexics, gets every month) is a big deal?

I'd do anything to undo what happened. I'm going to start wearing tampons every day of my life from now on. Or I would if it was safe, which I guess it isn't. I checked.

If I had a friend right now, I'd call her up. I'd talk her into doing something stupid, like smoking up or drinking. I'd talk her into doing something crazy, like climbing up onto the blue bridge downtown and dangling our feet over traffic.

Some days are worse than others, like today. Today it was seriously like I had my own personal force field. The boys are embarrassed by me. It's like they don't know where to look. Honestly, most of them stared at my crotch. Like I'll make *that* mistake again? Seriously. Jerks.

The girls (not just The Girls, but all of them) are out and out mean. I'm not stupid. I know what it's all about.

Self-protective. It's human nature, right? If the same thing had happened to them, they'd *die*. So by distancing themselves from me (like they were ever close), they avoid it themselves. Or something. What do I know? I just can't see my way out of it. I'm always going to be the girl who let her bleeding show.

I feel like I'm about to get a migraine, or maybe that's just from the regular I-have-my-period hormones or the more obvious head injury, I guess. In my vision, I'm getting those lights that drift by and spread, like my eyes are somehow slipping or melting or both. Even though I never take pills, I make my legs move and the mile and a half up to my parents' bathroom with the idea that I'll sneak a couple of sleeping pills from my parents' stash. I won't take them. But somehow the idea of having them in my pocket makes me feel like I could, if I wanted to. I don't know why. I've never done it before. I just need to do it right now. "Don't tell," I tell the velvet Elvis hung up over the toilet. I swear, he winks at me.

I'm losing my mind.

I jump out of my skin when my dad comes up behind me. He clears his throat. I can't hear him over my iPod, but I can feel him there somehow. The way he vibrates the air. The way he smells.

I grab the Tylenol instead of the others and shake it around. "Headache," I explain, without turning around.

"Hey," he says. He shifts back and forth a bit. "Hi."

"Hi, Dad," I say, popping out my earphone so I can actually hear him.

"Yeah," he says. "I was just going to … well. You know. Nature calls. And have a shower. Sweaty work."

He's looking someplace over my shoulder. Even my parents don't look me in the eye. Why?

The way he's standing there in these ancient rolled-up jeans, small belly sticking out under his dumb rock star T-shirt makes me either want to berate him for dressing like a child or poke him in the belly and laugh.

But I don't.

Dad is not the kind of person you do these things to, even though he seems like he would be. He's more of a distance person than a close-up-and-touching person. Unless it's Mum. He touches her all the time.

"Right," I say. "I was just ..." I let my voice trail off, knowing he won't ask. He "respects" me too much for that. Whatever. For a second, I think of this book I once read where the girl saw an island in the bottle of pills, swallowed them all to get there. I don't know what makes it jump into my head, but there it is. The Tylenols are like hard pebbles in my palm.

"You're okay?" he says.

"Yes," I lie.

"I never know what time it is," he says. "Did you eat?"

"I had an omelette," I say. "But I'll make something for you if you're hungry again."

"Yes, good," he says. "Maybe macaroni, okay? With some of those hot peppers if we have any?"

"Okay," I say.

My parents have always eaten like kids. Macaroni. Hot dogs. Tinned pasta.

"Okay," he says. His hands hover somewhere near his nose, like he's going to push up his glasses and then realizes he's not wearing them. Sometimes he looks so fragile.

He's not a person who seems like he could survive a fall from a bridge. Even one that isn't far from the water. I try to picture it, but I can't.

"If you want to talk, I always want to … talk, too," he says, shifting, like a little boy who needs to pee. "About school. I know high school is a nightmare. I hated high school. Wait until next year; you'll meet some better people. You'll have better … thoughts." I should walk away, only I don't. I'm in his way. Dumb. I should just move, but it's like I'm paralyzed, waiting for him to see me.

"Uh-huh," I say. "School is school. It's fine." I force my legs to bend and move. Leave the room so that I can breathe because suddenly, in that tiny bathroom, I can't. The air is used up.

I hear the shower go on. *Sure, Dad, school's good. I got an A on my biology test. A hundred percent. Do you care?*

I go into the kitchen and put a pot of water on to boil. I feel so restless. I swallow the Tylenol with tepid tap water that tastes like metal. I throw out the remains of the omelette and clean the pan. The lino is filthy and the bottoms of my feet are turning black. The windows steam up from the boiling water. I dump the noodles in the pot, stir them with a knife so they don't stick to the bottom. When it's done, I leave the pot on the sideboard for Dad to find, if he even remembers when he's done in the bathroom that he asked me to cook him something. I take a couple of bites myself, but I can't force myself to swallow. It tastes like hot plastic but also like something living. Tapeworms or amoebas or something worse.

I go for a walk outside just to get out of the stink of home. I feel so funny, like I'm about to faint or get sick. I don't like it, but I'm curious about the change. Is this like a hangover from the disappearance? Or does it mean that something else is going to happen? I feel like I'm waiting, holding my breath a bit, waiting for it to happen again.

I'm aware of my skin to the point where I can feel every pore. How my shaved leg stubble feels against my jeans. My T-shirt touching my belly and my back. I forgot my shoes, but it doesn't matter. It isn't cold, just fresh. And I like the feel of the sidewalk roughing up my bare feet. It makes me think of being a kid, always barefoot. It's spring, we should all be barefoot. We should all be touching the ground.

All through people's gardens, daffodils are tilting over, already almost done. Like yellow smears in the dirt, their stems too leggy and awkward to hold them up. I can smell them starting to decay.

I keep my eyes down so that I can see any glass or gum before I step on it. Music loud in my ears.

I walk for ages.

I pass my ugly school. A bunch of kids from my class are crowded around on the stairs, smoking. Don't they have homes? I pretend I can't see them. I pretend *they* are invisible. I'm glad I can't hear them. I can see one of them pointing at me, so I walk faster.

I pass the mall. I want to go in and grab a drink, but I feel too self-conscious with nothing on my feet. I mean, it seemed like a good idea to begin with, but now I just feel too visible. Besides, the mall probably has rules about being in there with no shoes, like No Shoes, No Shirt, No Service.

And I don't have any cash.

Just realizing that makes me parched. As I pass the parking lot, I can see people on their way to or from their cars staring at my feet. People who probably wouldn't notice my shoes, if I was wearing them. Like their eyes are drawn to what's different. I glare at them.

One woman says something to me that I can't hear. She has speckles of hairspray on her glasses. I pass her so closely I can smell the powdery smell of her makeup. I point at my earphones, and then I give her the finger. I don't know why. She looks so startled and hurt, I feel bad that I've done it.

The next building is the old bowling alley. It's empty and looks scary. The sign is half fallen off and one of the windows is broken. Funny how quickly empty buildings collapse. I can feel a different vibration under me now, like a pulse. Rhythmic.

Is it me? What is it?

I mute my music.

A basketball.

I follow the sound. My feet are filthy. I keep myself looking down. Looking for glass. There's lots of it around here. Why is there so much broken glass? Did people get together and decide that they would bring empty bottles here and smash them? Where does all this glass come from?

I light a clove cigarette and feel the burn in my throat. I cough.

With my earphones still in and the sound off, everything is muffled, but I can still hear the sound of the ball, feel it through my bare, cold feet.

I guess I knew all along it was Tony. If I really think about it, I was looking for him. I knew, sort of, that he'd be here. I know he's here a lot. I watch from around the corner so he can't see me, blowing my smoke down at the ground. He is mechanically shooting the ball into the hoop over and over again. Like a robot. From the same spot each time, it bounces back to him like it's magnetized. Past him, lying partway under a shrub that is growing through the wire fence, a bum of some sort is clapping. I stare at Tony, can't take my eyes off him. He appears completely enraptured with what he's doing. I'm mesmerized and also grossed out. He's sweating like crazy. Sprays of it come off him onto the ground.

Over and over again, the ball falls. It's so loud when it hits the backboard. I never thought of basketball as noisy. There's a cobweb dangling right over my head. I flinch and duck. I hate cobwebs. I hate it when they stick to me, those immovable threads.

Sticky things make me nervous.

My feet are so cold now. I slump to the ground, pick them up and inspect them. They're turning blue. A couple of pebbles look like they've embedded themselves under my skin. They feel like shards of glass. The sound of the basketball on the court is soothing, like music without all the clutter. It's making me feel very relaxed. Almost sleepy, as ridiculous as that sounds. Like the pills I didn't take are doing what they do anyway, like they have that power.

What if I fall asleep here? Then what? I force my eyes open and make myself breathe hard. This kind of sleepiness is great and terrifying. It's like an immovable force, rolling over me. Catching me. Grabbing me.

Eyes open. Open, open, open. I bite the skin on the inside of my cheek. Stay awake.

Stay awake.

The sound stops.

Quick, quick, quick as anything, before I can think about how to do it or why I'm doing it, I do *it*. I make myself disappear. In an instant, a heartbeat. Fade, fade, fade. *He can't see me watching him*, I think. *Too awkward. Stalkerish. Embarrassing.* Go, go, go.

Almost gone.

If I were to be honest, I sort of planned this without planning it. I guess I thought, *What if I could? What if I could watch without being seen? Then what?*

It sounds all wrong. It feels all wrong. But also it feels like I can't stop myself from doing it. I'd wanted to do it. And I did it. I know this. Just like I know that, if he saw me, I would die. Just like those silly, overly dramatic girls that I'm not. I would *die*. I'm too gross. He would be embarrassed to see me.

How else could he feel, being watched by the-girl-with-her-period, the-girl-with-the-weird-eyes? I'm sure that's all he knows me as. He wouldn't know me for any other reason.

I almost have to concentrate on staying faded. It's like I'm thinking it without being able to stop myself, getting darker, then lighter and then lighter still.

And I'm completely gone, shimmering. It feels like hard work, like my skull is too tight. My hair follicles too hot. Too cold. Both.

I can do it. I can do this. I can control this. I'm so surprised, I feel like I don't know if I should laugh or cry. I mean, think about it. I can spy.

It's gross. It's distasteful. But I know I'm going to do it. Like I have no choice, even though I know I do. I know I'm going to use it.

Without warning, the bum staggers to his feet and runs toward me. He's staring right at me. He claps. Laughing. Well, not laughing so much as grimacing and making a choking sound. Toppling.

"Are you all right?" It's Tony, approaching. I'm so close I can touch him but he can't see me.

I'm right *here*.

I'm not completely gone. I think I'm dark enough to see, if you really look. Sort of like a shadow. This time the burning-and-cold feeling was faster, so much faster than before. More intense. This time I'm aware of other things: my pulse, my breathing, the spinning in my head, the feeling that my fingernails are being tugged.

I'm aware that I feel papery and thin. Like if a breeze came up, it might actually blow me away.

I feel flammable. I drop my cigarette and leave it burning on the concrete, scared to step on it in case I ignite.

I feel like I can't possibly stay on the ground, like I'll float away.

I clear my throat, but no sound comes out. Interesting. I'm mute. So I don't just vanish, I'm silenced, as well. I say, "Tony." And he doesn't react.

I don't want him to see me, but I do.

I wonder, if I touched him, if he'd feel it. I want to. It's wrong, all wrong. It can't be the point of this. But ...

The bum suddenly kicks at him, makes a sound like a belch, flips him the bird.

"Whatever, man," says Tony. He has sweat pouring off his face, like in a commercial for a sports drink. "I lost count," he says. "I lost my place for you."

He dribbles the ball a bit. Whap, whap, whap. Takes off his sweatshirt, throws it hard in my direction. Runs back and forth across where centre court would be if there were any painted lines to see, his feet noisy on the blacktop. I cross to the other side, away from the tramp. There is a row of dumpsters, garbage spilling out. The ground feels so, so sharp under my feet. Sharper than before. That's strange, too. I'm both heavier and lighter. Inexplicable.

I pick the cleanest surface, so I can lean against the dumpster in the shadow of the most incredible maple tree I've ever seen. Bursting with its own green vividness. Leaves the size of flags. But when I do, the dumpster heats up against my skin and, just as quickly, starts to fade.

Creepy, creepy.

For a minute, I'm scared. My heart is beating like something trying to flap its wings in mud. An insect. *I* can make things disappear.

I touch the tree, but it stays solid.

Stays present.

I pick up a pebble, roll it between my fingers, but it's also still there. Hovering. I throw it hard, and it skitters under Tony's feet, but he doesn't notice.

Scary. I hold my knees and rock for a minute. I'm so torn. It's kind of cool, to be able to vanish. But making other things vanish? It's too much. What is *it*?

What am I?

What is happening to me?

The power is too much. Yet I wouldn't give it up now. It comes to me all at once: if someone could fix this, the truth is that I wouldn't want them to do it. Not yet. I'm not … done.

But still, there is something so sinister. So creepy about

this. So ... beyond *beyond*. Beyond bizarre. Maybe it's that I just don't understand it and I feel like I need to. I'm just completely overwhelmed by it, suddenly and powerfully, like when you're caught off-guard by a piece of music or something that just wrenches you open. I put my head down and cry. Why not? No one can see me or hear me.

I hardly ever cry.

It feels fake. Like I'm making it up. So I stop. A cat slinks by, leaps into the first dumpster. I can hear it in there, shifting rubbish.

I try to concentrate on Tony. He's still dribbling. Counting out loud. Fast. He gets to a hundred and whirls, quick as lightning, shoots the ball in.

He's so good.

I lie back and look up at the sky through the ceiling of leaves. I've never noticed this tree before. Not that I've ever been lying down behind the bowling alley either, so I guess that's not surprising. The tree is just amazing. It's *glowing*. The leaves are so bright and the wind is shifting them slowly. Yet they make so much noise. So colourful. It seems like when I can't see myself, I can see everything around me brighter. Hear things louder.

Maybe all of this, the trees, Tony, the bum, the alley, maybe they are all clues to some test that I'm taking without knowing I'm taking a test. Do I sound paranoid? I feel paranoid. Like this can't be something that's just happening to me. Someone must have done this *to* me. Someone must be observing. Probably I am supposed to be doing something now, but I don't know what it is. I'm letting someone down who may not even exist, that's what I feel like. Like I forgot to learn my lines and someone, somewhere, is really disappointed in my bad performance.

I frown. I feel so queasy, like carsick but more intense. And cold. Feverish. Hot. Tony bounces the ball hard against the backboard exactly ten times, hard. Ten more. I'm starting to notice a pattern. Ten of this. Ten of that. How long is he going to keep going? The bum has slumped over in a heap in no particular spot. He's either dead or asleep. I hope he's not dead. I don't think he is. Waves of alcohol come off him in rhythm with what can only be breathing.

I can't shake the feeling that I'm in a place where I shouldn't be, like any second now something terrible will happen that will somehow be my fault. Like I'm in a scary novel right before the killer strikes or the rabid dog appears from behind the building. A siren wails nearby, nearly causes me to have a stroke. It's like I'm so sensitive to sound that it actually lifts me up to my feet. The lights flashing by seem to ignite the entire sky.

The sun is setting.

I want to go home. I'm so tired. But I don't want to leave and the idea of walking home barefoot all that way suddenly seems too far. It *is* far. I wonder what time it is. The setting sun spills great splotches of colour across the cloudy sky. Which is when I get it in my head to hide in Tony's car. He only lives two blocks away from me. I can hitch a ride.

Can I?

My heart thuds hard, so hard. It's a balloon stretched so tight it's going to give. I'm scared, but I'm also excited.

What am I doing?

I can't remember the last time I felt like this. Maybe when I was little and it was my first time on the uneven bars and I looked down and it looked like I was so high up, I got vertigo that spun me around but also thrilled me.

It's like that.

Just about exactly like that.

Tony's throwing his sweatshirt back on. He's twirling the ball on his finger. He's getting ready. I have to do it. I brace myself, hold my breath, do all that I can think of to stay gone, like I have any idea what that is. I follow him a couple of steps behind. He's breathing loudly, hard and harsh. Soaked to the skin. His eyes are glittery, like he's been crying.

I want to touch his arm, just to see, but I'm not that brave.

A crow flies low, cawing, nearly flying through me (could it? I wonder) in its hurry to get to the dumpster. So loud.

Tony opens the door to his car. A hunk of rust falls to the ground. I hear it hit. The sounds remind me of when I have a migraine, just so tinny and sharp like they all have a razor-line shimmer around them. How can I get in? I can't sit *on* him. He'd see me for sure. I can see myself in the reflection of his side mirror, standing undecided. I can't see my face, but my body is definitely semi-visible. Tony isn't looking. He seems far away. Mad. He opens the back door to throw his stuff in and before I can think about it, I hurl myself in. He slams the door. I lie there just as I fell, heart beating so hard it's impossible to believe it won't burst. I'm panicking, I can't breathe,

I'm dizzy, I feel sick. Guilty. Strange. Wrong. I hold myself completely still; not that he'd notice if I didn't, but I feel paralyzed.

This is so much scarier than it would be if it was, say, a movie. In a movie, I wouldn't be afraid.

But what am I afraid of?

I'm mostly afraid I'm going to be sick. Or I'm going to fall asleep or faint. Or that if I stop concentrating so hard, I'll suddenly reappear.

Tony turns the radio on. He's talking to himself, mumbling under his breath. I can't make out what he's saying. After a commercial, a song blasts out. He starts to sing. It's an old, old song that I recognize from my parents' collection. It's the kind of music they like to play when they're working, like Led Zeppelin or Def Leppard or some other ancient rock hair band. He's *really* singing.

He can't sing.

I mean, it's the kind of singing you'd hate for anyone to witness. Embarrassing singing. I can't help it, I feel embarrassed for him. He hits a high note. Well, *misses* a high note.

I laugh. I don't mean to, it just comes out. He doesn't hear me. No, no, of course, he doesn't. I shift a little. Get more comfortable. He's still singing. I start to feel a little safer.

From where I'm lying, on the floor of the back seat, I can only see part of his profile. I see him sloop his hands through his sweaty hair and fling the sweat off in the general direction of his lap. Then suddenly he shouts, "Fuck!"

I gasp. Did he see me?

"Fuck," he says again. "Fuck you, Joe." Then he starts to cry. I mean, he's crying really, really hard. He's crying so hard that he turns into the wrong street and just stops the car. I've never heard anyone cry like that before. Never. I've never been so close to that kind of pain.

To tell you the truth, it makes me sort of fall in love with him but feel afraid of him and feel for him all at once. At least, I feel a falling sensation in my chest. A spinning and falling. He suddenly wrenches the door open and gets out. We aren't at his house. Where are we? He slams the door hard and I sit up enough to see him starting to run. He runs like he's being chased.

It's probably a good thing, because I look down and I can see myself. His basketball is digging into my lower back.

I'm back.

Oh God, that was close.

What if he had seen me? Then what?

I'm so hungry, I'm shaking. I feel like I haven't eaten forever. I feel like I have a fever. I feel like if I fade any harder than that, I might go away for good.

I somehow manage to open the door and get out. Race home, walking as fast as I can, mostly on lawns so my feet don't get more cut up than they already are. Slam into the house, tripping over the hall table. Crashing. Like I'm suddenly too big for myself. I'm excited and scared all at once, can't quite fit here in this place. Home.

"Saved you some macaroni!" Dad yells from downstairs.

"Thanks," I call back. My voice comes out like a croak. I take the plate of cold orange muck into my room with me. Play with it with my fork. But I'm too tired to eat. Collapse onto my bed.

I have the weirdest feeling. I feel ... almost, well, powerful.

I fall asleep so hard, it feels like falling off a bridge and smashing into something harder than water and splintering. Dreamless.

Empty.

Strong.

After all, I did it again. It's *real*. I can do it again. And I know I will. I have to. I can't stop now. Even though, maybe, I should.

TONY

5

IS THINKS WE should sign up for some stupid student council grad ski trip. He's totally pressuring me. I want to go, but I don't. This day isn't good. My back is sore: this morning the kid who sits behind me in the boat crabbed his oar and it jumped from his hand, smashing me hard in the spine. The bruise feels deep, like my back is made of metal that's being forced to bend the wrong way. My jaw is grinding from the pain, and from everything. Israel is getting on my nerves. He's jumping around me, clowning. I want him to stop. I just want him to shut up for a minute so I can think. Ski trip? No ski trip? Why does it feel like it matters so much?

"Come on," he says. "Dude. It'll be fun. It'll rock the house. It'll be the best. Oh, man. Spring skiing is the best."

"I don't know," I say. "I might have something. I have to check. There might be a regatta that weekend and I can't miss any more of those. I just can't."

"You can miss rowing," he squints. "I'm missing hockey. It's our last year of school! We're supposed to do this shit! If not now, when? Come *on*."

"Is," I say. "I don't feel like it. Give me a break, you asshole."

"You're the asshole," he says. "A boring asshole, too." He mock punches me in the jaw, and I duck out of the way. The pain in my back sings.

"Don't," I say. "My back is hurting." I lift my shirt and show him the bruise, which I know must be there.

"Wuss," he says, slapping it.

"Fuck you," I say. Shoving him into the wall. He laughs. But when he hit me, it really hurt.

Truth is, I don't really want to ski. I mean, skiing itself is okay, it's cool. Spring skiing kind of sucks, though, because the good snow is gone. It's more like skating, all that ice chattering under your skis. Nothing to grip. Too slippery, too fast, too out of control.

Well, mostly I don't want to go away for a weekend, leave my mum overnight.

What if something happens?

Like what?

I'm a kid. I *should* want to go on a ski trip.

"Give me a break, man," he says. "You've got to come. No choice."

I hesitate, and then scrawl my name under his on the sign-up sheet. I can't help but notice Michael's name on the sheet, too. I feel something like dread crawling on the skin on the back of my neck. Dumb. She's pretty and she likes me. So what?

"Hey, your girlfriend's gonna be there," says Is, as we make our way down the hall toward the biology lab.

"Ha ha," I say. "She's not my girlfriend." I jostle him a bit.

"Not yet," he says, pushing me back. He knows. I know. It's like some kind of fucked-up tide is bringing me and Michael together. Why fight it? I could do worse.

Skiing. Yeah, that's okay. I like to ski.

Mum will be fine. She's not my job. Right? I mean, I'm supposed to be having fun, aren't I?

I drop down into my desk, shoving my pack under my seat. Israel, beside me, is singing under his breath a rap song that I don't recognize. Tapping his desk with a pen. Papers are getting passed around. Tests are being returned.

I flunked.

God*damn*. I studied, too. It makes me mad that I failed. I think about that stupid science kit I'm always fooling around with. I can grow a crystal on my windowsill, why can't I do real science? Like adding stupid chemical equations?

I catch a glimpse of Yale's test as it gets passed to me down the row. She got a hundred percent. What the fuck? I wonder what that's like, to get a hundred percent in anything. Who knew she was smart? Other than Is, you don't get to be both smart and cool, which I guess explains why she isn't popular. She's pretty, so it's not that. She's like someone you always notice out of the corner of your eye but never really think about too much. She's ... different. I guess that's it. Different and, of course, totally shunned right now because of what happened at the last gymnastics thing. I don't know. I mean, I wasn't there.

I turn to give it to her. She's drawing something on the pale skin of her forearm, the ballpoint pen digging red into her flesh. She catches me looking, covers it up.

Like I care.

I glare at her.

She has the coolest, weirdest, freakiest eyes. Man. They make the hair on my arms stand up when she looks right at me. Spooky. Interesting. She really is hot in a weird waif-girl way. Huge eyes. I feel sorry for her, to tell you the truth. I want to say something like, "Man, sorry that happened to you," but it would come out wrong. She'd be mad probably.

Hostile.

She cracks her gum and it startles me. I turn back around. She's the kind of girl you don't really talk to very much. Except to say, "Here's your paper." Or, "Do you have a pen I can borrow?" It's like she's too much for this school. Too smart for sure. Too different. In a different world, she'd probably be admired.

Not here.

Still, she has that vibe, like she wouldn't give a shit about any of this if she were me. Just runs her fingers through her wispy hair and looks around the room like she has no idea how she came to be there and can't wait to leave. Her black freckles look almost blue they are so dark. They look like a map of the sky at night, in reverse. Dark on light.

She just doesn't care.

I want to not care. It would be better to not care. Then I wouldn't care about what Is is telling me right now — that Stasia finally hooked up with some jerk named Hooter at a party over the weekend. Hooter is an asshole. Rich, preppy, revolting creep. I want to find him and punch him. But instead, I laugh and say, "Lucky guy." Is looks at me strange, but so what?

"What?" I say. "She's hot. He's lucky."

"Yeah," he says. "If you have a crush on my sister, she is. You have a crush on my sister, Tony?"

"Nah," I say. "My heart belongs to Michael."

"Yeah, *right*," he says. "I believe that."

"Pipe down," says Mr. Morgenthal. "This is quiet study time, not shoot-the-breeze time."

"Sorry," Israel says. "We're studying."

"Sorry," I parrot. I make myself stare down at my stupid test. Forty-four percent. How can anyone get forty-four percent on anything? For a sickening second, my stomach drops and I can totally see clearly the future where I *am* my dad. Dumpy and dandruff-flaked and scurrying home to live with my mum when the going gets rough.

I shake it off. Tap my foot. Think about the game after school. Should be an easy one. We've never lost to MSS. Can't happen. They're all little short guys. Rich kids. Can't buy the genes to make them six foot two, though.

I'm kind of excited. I know I'm supposed to like a challenge, blah, blah, blah, but I like to win, too. And I know we will.

There's something nice about that. Comfortable. Makes the game fun.

My phone beeps, earning me another glare from Mr. M. It's Is. It says, **burgers downtown after game?** I shrug. I don't know if I feel like it. I'll probably go. Better than being at home. Better than TV. I should go for a run, go to the gym. But so what? I can skip a day. What could happen? I'll suddenly become out of shape overnight?

Not possible.

I have to remember how to relax. Since Joe died, I just *can't*. It's one thing that I've tried to talk about with Israel, something that I think he gets, which is why he tries to bully it out of me. It's just that I feel like I'm not supposed to. Or I'm not allowed. It doesn't make any sense, but what does?

Israel says that probably Joe would have been pissed with me for using him as an excuse, and he may be right. I wish he were right.

On one level, I think that Joe probably didn't care that much about me, but I don't say that. I don't say that to Is. I don't say that to anyone. I like the idea that he would have wanted me to keep going. I like the idea that he was that kind of person, after all.

I can remember feeling good. It used to come easily. Now it's like something inside me freezes sharp and hard, and I can't do it anymore. Israel is my lifeline. He notices. *He* cares, even though Joe probably wouldn't. He forces me to try.

Which is good, but also sometimes it makes me mad. Sometimes it makes me tired.

The weekend before school started, back in September, he totally dragged me out camping with a bunch of guys. It was mostly fun, I guess. Started off okay. We tubed on the river. It was freezing. But, yeah, I relaxed. I had a good time. For a while. Then a lot of guys drank until they puked, got stupid and loud and then passed out hard on the ground. That was too familiar. That was too much like Joe when the balance flipped for him between partying to have fun and partying as an excuse to drink and drink and drink some more.

I guess that ended the fun for me. I drank too much and cried. Since then, I've felt awkward around all of them. Outside of myself. I can't explain. I feel like I'm faking everything. Like I'm an old man who is just pretending to be a high school senior.

Luckily, I can just tell them I'm in training. No one ever tries to make me drink or anything. I do it voluntarily if I'm going to do it at all. It's not like on those PSAs where some kid's friends are always trying to make him drink or smoke or do drugs. Where do they find those kids? Seems to me that people do what they want. They have respect for people who don't. It's not all about, "Ooh, you have to try this or we won't like you." That's just bullshit. Never happens.

This morning, when I left for school, Mum was still asleep. She's been asleep for three days, I think. Her room is starting to smell like dirty sheets and greasy hair. She's missing so much work. How long will they let her get away with it?

I saw the number from The Bank on the call display about ten times. I hope she's called them back. I hope she's remembering to do that.

I mean, she wakes up to eat, but then just stumbles back to bed again. I guess she's "depressed." I've seen *Dr. Phil*. I know what's going on.

I just don't know how to fix it. Slip Prozac in her drinking water?

She's started smoking again. Hanging out of the bathroom window like a kid who's about to get caught. It gets all mixed up. Who is the kid? Which one of us can get into trouble? Isn't it supposed to be me? I don't care if she smokes. Maybe smoking will get her back together. Give her something to do with her hands so she stops freaking out.

Yeah, going downtown after the game would be okay. I

can grab a burger, not worry about dinner. Hang with my friends. Blend in. Be normal. There. The choice is made. Now I don't have to think about it. I can just think about the game. The win.

The points I'll score.

In the end, I get ten points, which I like. A nice even number, not a great score, but whatever. The roundness of it makes me happy. And we win, obviously. It's an easy win: fifty-three to thirty-eight.

Of course, because I have a car, a bunch of people pile in. Matti, Israel, Aurelia. Samantha in the front. Michael sitting on someone's lap in the back seat. She's looking at me in the mirror. She's smiling and stuff but I can tell it's an effort. She tries so hard. Sometimes I just want to tell her, "Look, it's okay. Stop trying." It makes me nervous. I kind of smile at her. I almost feel sorry for her. What does she want with me, anyway?

She's so focused on me, it makes her seem fierce, hungry.

I try to channel with my eyes, relax, relax, relax. It starts to rain a bit, windows are fogging up. People are horsing around. I can't see.

"Hey, T," says Matti. "Who've you been driving around in here?" He's holding something in his hand. What is it? Some kind of necklace? It's glass. It looks familiar, but I can't quite place it. I shrug.

"All you losers are always getting into my car because you can't drive," I point out. Getting my licence before everyone else has sort of turned me into the driver for everything. I don't care, I'm just saying. The necklace could be anyone's.

"Probably Stasia's," says Michael. She reaches for it.

She's laughing, but not laughing. She sounds bitchy, to tell you the truth. The way she says "Stasia." Like she's spitting, like a cat. How does she know about Stasia? I can tell that I'm blushing like an idiot.

"Stasia's never been in my car," I say. Israel snorts with laughter. Of course, it's a total lie. I'm not even sure why I said it; I've given Stasia a million rides. To make Michael feel better, I guess. Not that I have to do that. It's like Michael was saying, "You like Stasia better," and I was saying, "No, it's you, okay? It doesn't matter, I guess it's you."

"Wait," Aurelia says, grabbing it. "I've seen this before." She is swinging the necklace around. "I know whose this is." She gives me a look in the mirror. A hard look. "Huh," she says. "Surprise, surprise."

I still don't get it. "Whose is it?" I say impatiently. "What's the big deal?"

"It's Yale's," she says.

"Oh, The Bleeder," says Matti. "You been driving around with The Bleeder?"

"Don't call her that," I say, although I don't know why I feel like I have to defend her. "I've never driven her anywhere." This is true. I haven't. I feel confused.

Yale?

I feel something in my throat, like a spidery sensation. Like knowing something's wrong.

But that's just stupid. I mean, I don't even know the girl. I reach around and grab the necklace at the next stop light. Stuff it in my pocket. Sam and Aurelia are making some graphic and gross jokes. "What's white and red and spins around bars?" says one.

"Yale," says the other, laughing hard.

Michael doesn't laugh. She looks me in the eye. I like that she doesn't laugh. I don't know why I care, but I do. "I can give it to her," she says. "I'll return it."

She's got nice lips. Pearly. Smooth. Do girls condition their lips? Something about her lips seems extra smooth. They're probably soft. For a second, I'm lost in that thought. Like, really lost. I want to kiss her. I want to ...

"Kotex," screams Samantha.

"Just shut the fuck up," I say. And because I never talk like that, they all do. It starts to rain harder, which seems all the more strange because the sky is mostly blue. Somewhere there must be a rainbow, a bright one. But the rain is pouring off the glass so hard that I can hardly see at all anymore. Like I'm driving blind.

Michael

6

The fact that, after all this time, Tony made a move on her has Michael feeling both on top of the world and incredibly confused. Tony was her *unattainable* thing. Unattainable, as in safe. Unattainable, as in "not someone whose tongue will be lodged in my mouth at any time soon." Kissing scares her in a way that she'd love to admit to someone, anyone, if only anyone she knew was the kind of person she could actually confide in. She can't confide in any of The Girls. If they knew (if they ever thought about it, that is) how inexperienced she was compared to them (Aurelia has already had sex with four different people and the others regularly get drunk on the weekend and hook up with whoever at parties), they'd laugh at her. She'd lose all her power, if it is actually power that she has over them. Scarier still, she might lose their friendship, and then she'd be alone in the great sea of students, just another pretty face, and she wouldn't know how to be that person.

If Granny Aggie were still alive, she'd talk to her about it. About how her stomach clenched at the moment of lip contact (not in a good way, more in a please-go-away way) and everything inside her pulled back. Repulsed. Like he was somehow violating her in a way that was uninvited. But it was just a kiss. What is wrong with her?

The really painful part is that she had fantasized about that moment for so long, in so many different ways. She'd imagined that kissing him would be great. Magical. Transformative.

But it wasn't. Not even close.

For some reason, it also makes her not *like* him. It makes her mad at him, like it was his fault that one kiss didn't turn her instantly into a writhing, sensual heap, instead making her feel frozen inside. Locked up. Not how she wanted to feel.

How she deserved to feel.

He tasted like burger. Onions. But still ... it was *Tony*. Her Tony. This beautiful boy who she'd plotted to be with for so long and now she can't remember why. She has to rewind and remember, figure it out. Remind herself that this is what she *wanted*. What everyone *expected* because that is what she had set up to have happen, what she had planned and schemed and hoped for and imagined. It was her *dream*.

Maybe she had just been distracted by the taste — the horrible taste. Maybe that was all it was. She would never in a million, billion years allow herself to eat food like that. Greasy. Fattening. Skin-destroying. Revolting.

Not that making out with someone who ate that stuff was the same as eating it. Obviously.

The kiss also made her hyper-aware of the fact that her eye teeth were quite sharp, almost vampire-like, and when he thrust his tongue around in there she was almost afraid he'd get hurt. She also wondered about her own breath, probably terrible. She was instantly self-conscious, her insides curling like a salted slug from the horror of it. Bad breath from not eating being as bad (if not worse) than bad breath from eating gross things.

It didn't make sense, but even though she didn't enjoy it at all, not any of it, she wanted *him* to be enjoying it. She wanted him to want more, to love it. To love *her*.

And also to never touch her again.

She'd had plans, that was the hard part. He was going to be The One. Her first. She'd planned it for so long she didn't know how to re-imagine the plan. But if the kiss was so … bad. The real thing wouldn't be good either.

Maybe there was something wrong with her?

She could follow through, anyway. It wasn't just about kissing. It was about being with him. Being Tony's girl. Being safe in that. Because he's *Tony*, he's so nice. And gorgeous. And everything, obviously, that she's ever wanted.

But, still, there was that feeling. That bad feeling. That feeling of being humiliated. But why? Tony would never humiliate her. That was part of why she'd picked him to begin with: his inherent kindness. The way his eyes smiled when his lips did. The way he never looked away from her face when she spoke. The way she knew he'd never brag or talk about her or any of that.

Afterward, Israel sneaking him a high-five like she wouldn't notice. Israel, the opposite of Tony, full of locker-room gossip. Like a girl, but trashier. Meaner. All hard edges and brash cruelty. Much like Aurelia, come to think of it. A male version.

Tony awkwardly getting out of the car to hug her when he dropped her off. She could tell he wanted to kiss her again, but she'd turned her head to the side, buried her nose in his shoulder instead. Smelling the reassuring smell of him. Avoiding the wet lips, the slippery tongue, the too-much saliva.

Aurelia frantically making the "Call me!" sign. Sam glowering, but Sam had a crush on him, too. She should have known that. Why hadn't she noticed it before? She made a half-smile at Sam, raised her hand to Aurelia, let go of Tony.

She wanted to redo it. Start from the top. Chew some mint gum, maybe that was all the problem was. Give him gum before he swooped in with his lips like a bird of prey lunging at a mouse.

It was all mixed up somehow with Yale's necklace. She said she'd give it back to her and he'd handed it over, relief in his eyes (was he scared of Yale himself?) as though obviously Michael would see Yale before he'd see her. Yet he must have known they weren't friends, that Yale wasn't a girl who had friends, or maybe he's just a boy and unobservant and oblivious like they all are.

She'll give it back, of course. Michael looks up as Tony's car finally pulls away, disappears down the street. She holds the necklace up in front of the porch light, which is always on because no one can figure out how to switch off the sensor. The glass pendant is big, pretty, strange. Full of greens and blues, sort of like the whole world encased in glass. Like a marble. Sully would love it.

If she showed it to him, he'd hold it tight and never let it go, so she can't do that. Can't even let him sneak a peek. Maybe she should just give it to him, pretend she doesn't know about it, but no. It's Yale's. She'll give it back. She holds it against her cheek; it's cool. It's not something she would ever wear herself. Too hippie. Too alternative. Too out-of-the-ordinary. Too *too*.

But somehow mesmerizing.

Hard to look away from. The glass has more and more colours the more you look at it. Little patterns that you don't see at first. It almost looks alive, like inside it is moving.

Frankly, she's a little surprised that Yale would wear it. But what does she know about Yale? She never really pays much attention to what Yale is wearing. She really only worries about her own clothes, her own look. Always perfect. Always chosen so carefully, everything matched to look both unmatched and yet right, like it's her job or something. She barely sees other peoples' outfits unless they are wearing something incredibly great or something incredibly awful. When she thinks about it, she can't picture Yale in anything except jeans and T-shirts (and gym clothes, of course). And the necklace. She never would have remembered the necklace in describing Yale, but now that it's in her hands, she realizes she has never really seen Yale without it.

They've been on the same teams and at the same schools forever, but no one even knows Yale, she thinks. Come to think of it, Yale has always been alone. Never with a friend or attached to a group or anything. Almost like she does it on purpose, acts all mysterious and secretive to keep people away. Better than everyone else. Not willing to do the things everyone else does to fit in, like make herself look her best. Make her smile whiter, her hair straighter, her skin look clearer. Like she's above all that.

Or maybe Yale is more like every monster in every movie ever made. Weird-looking and off-putting in some mysterious and yet not totally heinous way. But maybe, under it all, a heart of gold.

Much like Michael herself is misunderstood. Assumed to be one way, because of the way she looks. Not feeling the way she *should* feel.

Not feeling anything really at all.

Maybe Yale would get that. Probably she would. Strangely enough, Michael feels an overwhelming urge to go inside and call her up. Act like they *are* friends. Confide in her in a way that she'd never confide in, say, Madison, with her fake accent and her constant name-dropping and celebrity obsessions. Confide in her like a real friend. Like a real person, not just a person who seems like they're always acting, like Sam. Aurelia. Like Michael herself, really, if she thinks about it.

She stands outside. Unmoving. Under the sign that's swinging in the warm spring breeze. Now that the rain has stopped, the air smells delicious: almost like summer, like wet grass and rising warmth and earth. She breathes so deeply she almost falls over, knocks her head on the sign. The sign that says ANIMAL TAXIDERMY. A picture of a fox, staring, beside the printed phone number. The fox is ugly. As far as she can remember, her parents have never actually done a fox. Lots of family dogs. She shudders. She will never, ever own a dog. Nothing furry. Nothing *not* furry either, come to think of it. Reptiles are as bad, if not worse.

Why is she thinking about this now?

She should be thinking about Tony. Is he going to call her? Does this mean that they are together or is it casual?

Why doesn't she feel something other than just queasy and even maybe a bit victorious?

She'll go inside, she decides. The wind is blowing her hair everywhere and making a mess. She'll deep condition and maybe meditate. She'll figure it out. She'll call Aurelia. Aurelia will say the right thing. Actually, Aurelia probably won't say anything useful but talking to her is sort of like reading trashy books or watching romantic comedies. It's light. Distracting. Takes her mind off things.

Maybe she *should* call Yale. Not to talk, that was a stupid idea. Just to tell her she has the necklace. See if Yale says anything about Tony.

No.

She opens the door to the sound of a symphony being played at full volume. Angene and Chelsea are all decked out in crazy scuba outfits, frolicking with some kind of stuffed fish. A guy she's never seen before with wild red hair and a beard is snapping pictures.

"Hey gorgeous," he says. His eyes drift up and down her in a way that makes her shudder. Makes her want to go put on more layers of clothes. A turtleneck. He all but wolf-whistles. Tongue hanging out. Disgusting.

She nearly gags. He has visible dandruff flakes on his shoulder.

"Yeah," she says. "Hi." Cuts him dead with her best, I'm-fantastic-and-you're-a-gross-pig look.

"Your sister's ... wow. Pretty," she hears him say as she goes up the stairs.

"Yeah," says Chelsea (or is it Angene?). "But she's a little bitch."

Michael sticks her head into Sully's room. He's sitting in the middle of the floor, lining up Hot Wheels in a circle around him. He only has red cars. No other colour is okay. She gave him a green one once and he threw it out the window. In his eyes, she'd read that she had let him down. They conveyed something close to betrayal. Or maybe she imagined that.

"Hey gorgeous," she says softly, repeating the photographer's words, only she means it. Sully doesn't turn around, but carefully straightens one of the cars. He doesn't look up, but his shoulders tilt in her direction.

"Guess what?" she says. "I kissed Tony Nelson. For real. He kissed me. What do you think?"

His shoulders lift. Maybe they do. Maybe he's just moving to see the cars in the beam of his flashlight that he always has by his side.

"I didn't much like it," she whispers. "I thought it was gross."

Still no reaction. She feels like crying.

"It was awful," she goes on. "I hated it. But I like *him*. What's wrong with me? What is it?"

Nothing. A Hot Wheels car shoots out of his hand and bangs into the leg of a chair. She bends over and rolls it back over to him.

"See you later, doll," she says. Because really, that's what he's like. A doll. A doll that sometimes freaks out, but most of the time is just placid. Just *there*. "Thanks for listening."

Michael wishes ... well, she wishes he were a normal big brother. With cool friends that she could hang with.

Wishes she could have a conversation with him, that he'd answer. Wishes that it were different. And yet she'd never wish him away. By wishing he were different, she's sort of wishing he (as he is now) didn't exist, and that makes her feel terrible. She loves Sully so much. But still, an older brother who could interact and laugh and all those things? Well. She's just sad for him, that he can't do those things. But, then again, maybe he doesn't want to. Maybe he's happy, just not in the same way as her sisters. Not in such a *loud*, show-offy way. There's nothing to say that being quietly happy is worse or better than being as obnoxious about it as they are.

Her head is starting to ache.

While she's on the topic of wishes, she also wishes she had a home with a regular living room, not a large white box more often than not being used as a studio by her sisters and their freak friends. Boxes line the hall all the way to her room; Mum and Dad must have a big order shipping out. Her skin ripples with gooseflesh when she thinks about what might be in the boxes. Like creepy animal coffins.

She'll do her nails, too. Hair, nails, meditate. Then maybe homework. She has to ice her knee, which she twisted this morning at practice doing a totally simple walkover, a move she's been able to do since she was three. Clumsy. She can tell it's maybe almost beginning to swell. A twinge when she steps hard on that leg. A tingle.

Then, after all that, she'll take a bath. *Then* maybe she'll have figured out all this stuff about Tony. Already the kiss is starting to seem like something she made up in her head, not like something that actually happened. Not like something real.

Which is good, because then maybe she'll be able to think of it differently. That's probably the best. To start talking about it. She'll call Sam and tell her about it. She'll tell her it was incredible. She'll tell Sam she felt it in the soles of her feet. She'll call Aurelia and say the same. And Madison. And then, probably, after all that, that will be the truth.

Then it will be okay. He can still be The One. Because she so badly wants it to be Tony with his gentle eyes and his sheepishness and his ... well, his lack of fierceness. His lack of manliness. That may sound weird, and she'd never say it out loud, but it's true.

She goes down to the kitchen for a glass of water. Her sisters are intertwined on the floor. Gross. Even if she wanted to talk to one of them about it, it wouldn't fly. They're both basically sluts as far as she can tell. A different boyfriend every month. They buy condoms at Costco. They are so easy in their own skins, so free to show everyone everything they have. They aren't like her at all. They would never ever in a million years understand.

As she watches, Angene reaches out and tickles Chelsea, like they are toddlers and not adult women. They are trying not to laugh or trying to laugh, it's hard to tell which. The camera shutter is snapping. Snapping. Snapping. The flaky-skinned photographer smiling with his crooked yellow teeth showing, looking not unlike a feral animal himself. Snap, snap, snap.

"Stop!" she wants to scream. But she doesn't know why. The sound of the camera is hurting her ears.

Well.

What are her sisters trying to prove? Why are they so *happy*, anyway?

They should get real jobs. Madison's older sisters work at Sephora, and she gets great deals on makeup. Aurelia's sister is a hairstylist, so Aurelia gets highlights for free. And what does Michael get from her sisters? Total waves of humiliation, that's what. Free embarrassment. A cringe-a-day. A discount on reasons-to-hide-your-face-in-public.

Why do they have to be so *weird*? Don't they know it makes it hard for her to be so perfect? So perfectly normal?

Don't they know how hard she works at being okay?

Don't they *care*?

Yale

7

The more I do *it*, the easier it is. Not just physically, but that's true, too. I can make myself vanish now just by thinking it into happening. Concentrating. I can't explain how; if I think about *how*, it stops working. If I turn off my conscious thoughts, it's like I can actually *control* everything, every cell in my body, every part of me.

Mostly, I do it in my room. Alone. In front of the mirror, like I'm practising smiling for my school pictures except obviously not like that at all. After hours of practice, hundreds of times, I can fade from left to right, right to left. Top to bottom. I can make only my hand disappear.

It's so intense. I can't even fully describe it. It's unbelievable. And, I have to admit, uncomfortable.

Still, I feel like I've won something. More than that. That it means something huge. That it means that I'm something special after all. Something really special.

Is this what I've wanted all this time?

The more I do it, the more it seems *normal*.

The more it seems fun.

Surreal, sure. Slightly painful. But fun.

Then, out of the blue, I suddenly know that she can do it, too, the other Yale. I know it in some fundamental way, like I know what colour a flower is even when I smell it with my eyes closed. I just *know*.

Last night I dreamed about her, about my sister. I dreamed that she was alive, so I think that means that she is. I couldn't see her though. It was like she was there, but she wasn't. I'm going to ask Mum. Today. I am.

I'm just working up the strength. It's funny, when I think about saying something, I can hear my voice frogging up. My muscles feel like rubber bands. But what am I so afraid of? What's the worst that she can say?

Well.

The worst would be that she, that Yale, was dead. That would be the worst. So when I rehearse the conversation in my head, I give Mum that line. "She's dead." I've imagined her saying it so many times that I think it wouldn't hurt me now. Not as much as if I were unprepared.

I take a deep breath of dust-laden air and hold it until I sneeze. The sun reflected in the mirror glances off my eyes sharply. I disappear one more time, for good measure, and then reappear and force myself to go downstairs. If I don't ask now, then when?

And why shouldn't I?

Mum is at the kitchen table drinking a tall glass of chocolate milk through a straw and cutting individual slices from an apple with a sharp paring knife. She concentrates on it so fully that she doesn't look up when I enter the room. I fling the fridge open so the door bangs into the table, which is positioned too close in the small room.

"Careful," she says automatically.

"Sorry," I say.

I stare into the fridge. Milk, juice, eggs, cheese, a wilted head of lettuce. I'm not hungry, anyway. The light inside blinks and goes out. It's a sign, probably, but of what?

Of a dead light bulb, that's what. Nothing more.

"I need you to tell me what happened to Yale," I say all at once, just as the clock in the living room starts to chime. I think I say the words too fast, that she can't understand me. She doesn't look up, but carves another perfect slice off the apple, raises it to her chapped lips, chews. Swallows.

I clear my throat and think about saying it again.

"I …" I start.

"Who told you about Yale?" she says. "I knew it would come up eventually."

"You did," I say. "I mean, it was in your blog."

"You read my blog?" She squints at me. Takes off her glasses and rubs them on her shirt, smearing fingerprints around before replacing them on her face. "Huh."

"Huh," I echo.

"Well," she says.

"Well," I say. My head is spinning a bit and I feel like I might fall over, so I lean on the counter. An edge of Arborite has come loose and I stick my finger underneath it. Feel the sharp border with my nail. I close my eyes.

"Yale," says my mum.

"That's me," I said. "But also, her."

"I know," she says. "I don't like to talk about it."

"Sorry," I say, not meaning it.

"She's not well," she says. "She's just not well. She's ... She's got a lot of ... She's ..."

"She's alive," I say, flatly.

"Yes," she says. "She is being taken care of."

"By who?" I say. The skin behind my nail starts to bleed from the pressure. I pull my hand away.

"Oh," she says vaguely. "She's ..."

The front door slams open. With surprising speed, my mum's face whips around to mine. "We can talk about it another time," she says. "About her."

"Oh," I say. And before I can come up with more of a reply, my mum is gone. The paring knife sitting on the table. For a second, I almost think she disappeared, she used my trick. My thing. But then I hear her footsteps in the hall, going down the stairs.

Dad walks by and says, "Hey," before following her. I hear their voices rise and fall. I could go down there, I think. I could listen to what they are saying. But I can't. I feel glued into place. She's got a lot of *what*?

At least she's alive.

At least I know that now for sure.

I think.

I reopen the fridge and grab the old wilting lettuce, slice it into chunks and gnaw on one like a rabbit. Sure, I know it's weird, but I like to eat lettuce this way. This one is a little past its prime. Not so juicy. But still good.

I feel like a rabbit.

I chew and swallow. Chew and swallow.

She's alive. Now what?

I go upstairs and crawl under the covers, fully dressed. Finish the lettuce. Close my eyes and try to think.

The compulsion to spy is so strong. I know I'm going to do it again. What I can't decide is exactly how wrong it is. If no one knows, am I hurting them? Really hurting them? And if they aren't hurt, is it still wrong? Well, it's obviously wrong, but relative to what? It's definitely morally wrong, I know that from the squeamish feeling it gives me. But is it, like, criminal?

I'd hate it if someone did it to me. But …

I'm curious, although that isn't a strong enough word. It's like I have to know now more than ever what goes on in other people's lives because it seems like I suddenly have a way to fulfill all that curiosity. It's like something bigger than me bubbling up in me. I can't help thinking, *I could just go* look. Maybe I'd figure something out, like why I can't fit in. Maybe I'd figure out what everyone else does that makes them so normal and me so … not.

If you think about it, this is incredible. It's sort of like an all-access pass. Apart for the small complication that, when I fade, I don't vanish altogether. It could be risky. But then again, I did it in a gym full of people and no one saw me leave.

It's like they *can't* see me, even though I know they could if they looked hard enough. They *won't* see. As if I'm protected by their fear of what they don't understand. Their inability to comprehend makes them blind.

I sit up and push the covers back and watch my arm vanish. Goosebumps appear and then are gone, camouflaged by my lumpy bedspread. I don't exist. All around me, the colours deepen, like I've turned up a saturate button. Too bright. I get up noisily but also soundlessly. As in, I know that I'm the only one who can hear it. I jump up and down. Hard, on the floor.

Nothing.

I'm going to try something. If not here, where's a better place? Hiding in my own home. It's like a test. I make my way slowly down the hall toward the kitchen, where Dad is making peanut butter toast. Pretty much his staple diet. He spreads the peanut butter on so carefully, from corner to corner. I move closer. And then closer still. How close can I get? I am right behind him. I am almost touching him, my arm brushing the fabric of his sleeve. The peanut smell is so strong, I can practically taste it, my mouth feels sticky. Glued shut. He doesn't look up from his meal, looking at it so closely it is like he is inspecting it for lice. I reach out and touch the knife that he was using and it, too, vanishes. He doesn't see.

He doesn't notice.

My heart is pumping hard. It's almost too powerful and too dumb to be using that power to just look at people, especially to look at my dad, inhaling the toast without chewing. If I were someone better, maybe I'd know what else to do with this crazy gift. But I'm not.

I'm just me.

I go back to my room. I'm nervous for some reason. I know I'm not going to be able to stop. I think that's what scares me, my own drive to do this thing that I know is wrong no matter how I shape it and reshape it in my head. I sit down. I feel restless but also like I can't take the next step. I fade in and out from my head to my feet and back. I feel like I have a terrible fever. I wish the hot and cold didn't happen. I have to stop myself from doing it just randomly. It's like when you have a sore in your mouth and you can't stop touching it with your tongue, even though you know you shouldn't. I can't stop.

It seems like such a short distance between being me, normal old me, and being this other person, this person who wants to watch other people, this voyeur. This creep. It's too easy. It's too ... appalling. I find this so depressing that I pull the covers back up and turn out the light. It's too bright, though it's only late afternoon. The sun is pouring in through the window like a cheerful kid, pestering me. Stopping me from sleeping or hiding. Dust particles dance in the rays of light.

I love the weight of the blankets: it makes me feel like everything's going to be okay. I force myself to think about something else and what pops into my mind is gymnastics practice this morning. It went okay, generally. Nothing thrilling. Nothing happened. The gym smelled, as always, of rubber-soled shoes, chalk and sweat. We did some drills and stretches. I concentrated on perfecting my dismount from the beam. I bruised my shin, but that's nothing new; I'm always bruised and battered.

I'm getting used to the weird new way my eyes seem to work. I'm getting used to my new body. I'm getting ... well, better. Being able to see more, being more aware makes me more accurate. Makes me really, *really* good.

Not that anyone has noticed.

We talked about the next meet. I tried to block out any mention of the *last* meet, because obviously everyone was thinking about my stupid period. To be honest, I felt really sick. Dizzy. I was waiting for Aurelia to make a crack. Waiting for Madison to snicker. Waiting for Sam to roll her eyes. I had to concentrate on *not* disappearing, because when you're in a group of five people, they'll definitely notice when you suddenly evaporate.

I got through it. Basically, we just decided that Coach

would make all the decisions about who did what routine. We weren't specific. There was only one moment when Aurelia suggested that we wear our red bodysuits that made me die a little inside. I counted slowly in my head. Concentrated on my own pulse. Steady, steady.

Then, out of the blue, Michael said, "Hey, Yale, you left this," and passed me my necklace.

"Uh," I said.

"Yeah, you forgot it. In *Tony's* car." She fixed me with a look that I couldn't read. Quizzical. Curious.

"Oh!" I said. "Um." Did she know? She knew. She did. Her blue eyes didn't leave my face. What was she thinking? "Thanks," I mumbled.

My heart was racing. I started to see stars. *Breathe*, I reminded myself. *Breathe*. Now would not be a good time to faint. I focused in on whatever I could: sounds. I could hear the clock ticking loudly. Someone's shoe squeaked and a cell phone rang loudly somewhere outside the gym.

"So," I said. "That was nice of you to give it back." I clenched the necklace in my hand. She stared at me. She had a funny half-smile on her face. The glass was cool and smooth, like a fist full of still water. Then I turned around and ran to the showers. My shoelaces were untied and rained down on the floor like a dog's claws scrabbling.

"Hey, wait!" she called after me. But I pretended not to hear. It was just easier that way.

Now, from my new under-the-blankets perspective, I realize that there are a hundred things I could have said. I could have pretended to not understand how it got there. I could have said I'd loaned it to someone who might have more obviously been in Tony's car. I could have said it wasn't mine, but I wanted it back. I loved that necklace although I couldn't recall where it came from or why I always wore it. It must have been a gift from my parents; I don't get anything from anyone else, and I'd never buy anything like it for myself. Swirls of falling colour trapped in glass.

I could have said anything. Not saying anything must have just made me seem even stranger to her, so much less than normal. Less than her. Why couldn't I have been casual? Chatty? Nice?

Why did I make everything so hard? I wonder, after all, what she does think of me. She must think something, even if it's just, "God, that girl is so *weird*."

I take a deep breath and hold it. I play with the necklace, which now hangs around my neck where it always has. How did I not notice it was gone?

I frown.

It's hot under the blankets. Like breathing air in a sauna, it's damp and sticky. I'm sweating.

I want to go outside. I need to go outside. I want fresh air. Cold, fresh air. Fresh air and trees and green grass to inhale.

When I go downstairs, I can hear the murmur of Mum and Dad's voices.

I hesitate by the phone in the front hall. I could call someone. Who? Anika? No. I can't think of a single person who wouldn't be really surprised to hear from me. I can picture the awkward silence while they wait for me to say what I want. I can imagine them wishing they hadn't picked up.

I fish around in the hall closet and find my coat. Stick

my bare feet into some old gumboots. Propel myself out the door, shouting, "Going for a walk!" down the basement stairs.

I'm out on the street. Hurrying. My bare feet loosely rubbing inside the too-big rubber boots. I'm hyper-aware of everything. The colour of the sky, quickly turning into a deep purplish blue. The huge bright moon rising through the rooftops. Puffs of exhaust as cars and buses trickle by. A waft of dog poop as I pass the Crazy Lady's house. The Crazy Lady has about twenty little fluffy dogs, matted and filthy, encrusted with their own waste.

I'll never be like that.

Some dogs spill out onto the lawn. I walk faster, cross the street. I'm sweating under my coat, so I take it off. I wanted cold fresh air, not this summer-like thick warmth. It's too suffocating.

The street is deserted. Except for me. Not a lot of people seem to go for evening walks. Why not? In tiny strange patches, as random as the warm patches you find when you swim in the ocean, I get what I want: the air is so sweet and clear, like fresh cold lemonade. As I make my way by house after house, I can see the flicker of TV screens. People hunched over computers. It gets darker and some streetlights hum to life. A flurry of birds' wings as a startled flock abandons a wormy-looking lawn.

No cars in sight, no one on the road but me. It's my chance and I catch my breath and do it. Step one: fade away. A ripple of goosebumps and then heat and I'm gone.

I think at first that I'll start with just peeking in windows or something. Something innocuous. Innocent.

Something ... that seems okay. Or at least something where I wouldn't actually be breaking any laws. Although do laws apply to the invisible?

I don't know.

But no. I am in front of Michael's house. Step two. It's not an accident, not at all. I think of how she looked at me this morning. Her perfect hair like fine Christmas tinsel glimmering around her shoulders. Her eyes sparkling. Her funny smile, like she *knows* something. What does *she* know?

Bitch.

Yet, also, I sort of want to tell her. I don't know why. What is it about her?

Crazy, crazy, crazy.

Who do I think I am?

Step three. Michael's house. The sliding glass door is partly open, and I am inside her house before I have a chance to change my mind. I guess it would be easier if I could just pass through solid objects, but I can't. It's noisy when I open it, but I pause in the doorway and no one seems to hear or care. There are voices upstairs, but the room I am in is completely empty except for a few spotlights and some photography equipment. It's effectively a big white box. No shadows to hide in, to cover me up. I'm so scared.

So scared. My heart is going to erupt. I feel like I might be sick or I might laugh or wet my pants. Or all three.

Why am I doing this? Quickly, so quickly, I make myself move. Head for the stairs, the only visible option out of this weird place. As I move up the stairs, I notice that along the walls animal heads are staring out at me.

It's seriously creepy. Like something from a bad movie or the set of a Halloween prank. It makes me think differently of Michael, I can tell you that.

My hand touches a stuffed squirrel on the railing, which disappears on contact, causing me to scream. But silently, I have to assume. No one comes running. It's okay. I exhale. I'm still safe.

I duck into the first open doorway. It's a bedroom. No one in it. A few stuffed dead animals lying around that look like an assortment of family pets, frozen in time. Well, except for the dog tipped over in mid-run. He just looks dead. Marble eyes that I can't help but notice are much like mine, one brownish, one blue.

Gross.

Some photos are scattered on the bed. I can see a lot of flesh in the pictures. Girls. What kind of weird place is this? What am I doing here? Is this really Michael's home or did I get it wrong? The carpet is shag, circa 1970. Olive green. It looks like seaweed. There is a smell in the air that I can't pinpoint. Maybe it's the animal fur. It's a thick smell, an acrid musky smell.

In the next room — the door is ajar — a boy (or is it a man? He's tall, it's hard to tell) is sitting on the floor. No, he's not really a boy, he looks older than me. But he also looks like a baby. His skin is so smooth, it's mesmerizing. I really want to touch it. For a minute I think he's a wax figure, the way he's just staring into the corner of the ceiling, a book open on his lap.

His hand moves.

He scares me. I'm scared. This place is nothing like what I imagined. Nothing like the regular suburban house it is on the outside. It's so strange in here; the light moving through the air is different. The odour, definitely. The sounds echo and feel staged. Everything looks different than I expected.

It's like that moment when you see the girl in the bikini going into the cabin in the woods. "Don't do it!" you want to scream.

Only I'm already here.

I hear footsteps passing. Instinctively, I get into the closet like a little kid playing hide-and-go-seek. There is a row of T-shirts on hangers. Who hangs up their T-shirts?

I press myself as deeply as I can between them. I can't trust the invisibility. I feel like it can't be real, even though I know it is; it doesn't matter. My heart is pounding so hard I feel like it should be shaking the ground. The wall feels solid against my back. I'm burning hot from the vanishing. *Breathe*, I think. Just as I hear someone say, "Breathe."

I jump. Nearly give myself away by knocking over a pile of white sneakers. So many shoes in here, the smell is strong and fetid and sweaty and nearly overpoweringly boyish.

"Breathe."

It's Michael's voice. Coming from the other side of the wall. This closet must somehow back onto her room.

"Don't be so crazy," Michael's disembodied voice says. "Stop thinking about it. Stop thinking about him." She's speaking so loudly. Like she's talking to a microphone.

"If he didn't eat those onions," she says. "If I had better breath. If. Then. I'd be okay. It was just a kiss. Why am I making it such a big deal?"

"Just a kiss. Not anything more. Nothing scary."

"It wasn't too much."

"Come on. It was fine."

No one answers. She's talking to herself. Well, that's okay. Who doesn't? I do it all the time.

"Just breathe," she says. "Get over it."

I get out of the closet. The boy-man looks at me, but he couldn't. He can't see me. I wave, but he doesn't respond. See? There's something wrong with him. He's not okay.

I wonder if he is the same sort of not okay as Yale. My sister is also "not okay."

Well.

I don't know, do I?

I don't know anything. I look back at him. He's staring right at me. I walk toward the window and his eyes follow. He doesn't seem to care, though.

"Well, bye, then," I say. "Nice to meet you." I know he can't hear me, but still, he closes his eyes, like he's absorbing the information. There's something about him. I almost want to stay.

I step into the hall. I'm at the next door, which must be Michael's room, but it's shut. The house echoes with a feeling of fundamental emptiness, yet coming from what must be the kitchen, I still hear voices and sounds. I smell something cooking, something that doesn't smell good. Cooking spinach maybe or cabbage soup. I'm scared to go in that direction, and besides, the glass French door is closed. If I were to open it, someone would definitely notice.

The door I want to open is Michael's. I want to see her, which *sounds* creepier than it feels, I swear. It feels okay. It feels … innocent somehow. Almost as if I'm simply watching a film. Or doing research. Gathering information.

Stuff to know about Michael. Stuff that might help me to be more like her, or get her to like me. It sounds all wrong when I say it, but that's what I'm thinking. I'm thinking that there is some secret here for me to learn.

"Michael!" I hear a voice yell from somewhere behind me. I'm afraid to look. She doesn't answer. My heart is erupting. A volcano of adrenalin pumps through my veins. I swear I can feel it. Taste it like copper in my mouth. "MIKE!"

"Don't *call* me that!" she shouts back.

"Dinner's almost READY," says the other voice. Her mum? Her sister?

"FINE," she yells.

I just stand there. The carpet fibres feel like crunchy plastic under my feet, too synthetic for words. Maybe that's part of the smell, the overriding chemical odour. The hall is lined with class pictures of Michael and her older sisters all in identical black frames. I remember now that she has sisters. When we were really small kids, I remember going to gymnastics class after school and Michael's sisters were in the more advanced group. They were so alike, it was creepy. From the pictures, it looks like they still are, except one of them has shrunk and one of them has plumped up. And, well, one of them is bald.

I touch my hair, which feels like I'm touching feathers. Wispy, insubstantial.

To be bald must feel very ... I don't know. *Vulnerable* is the only thing that comes to mind. The sister's head in the picture reminds me of a baby bird. It's obviously the most recent picture because the photos are lined up in chrono-logical order, the girls growing up as you move down the hall. This last picture shows the sisters on some kind of stage. They are wearing fur coats. It looks like bright lights are shining in their eyes because they are both squinting and their eyes glow red like embers.

It's amazing how you can know someone for your whole life and not know them. Knowing that they live with a picture of themselves in the third grade, hair askew, wearing a plaid jumper, somehow changes something. Knowing about their sisters. Their brother.

Michael suddenly swings her door open hard, moves past me into the room I just left. Her brother's room. I hold my breath, flatten myself along the wall like a limpet, not really knowing why. It wouldn't help, not if someone looked right at me. My head knocks crooked a picture showing their dad drinking generic brand beer (a bright yellow can labelled BEER!). I pick it up and replace it. Her dad (I assume that's who it is) drinks BEER! a lot, from the look of these pictures, a can in his hand as the years float by on the wall.

"Sully, Sully, Sully," I hear Michael singing. "Time to eat, time for a feast of stewed tofu or bug soup. You'll like it, big brother of mine. And you know, if you don't, we'll sneak some peanut butter toast, you and me." There are a few thuds, like he's rocking the legs of his chair back and forth. I wish I could see them but I don't want to get too close.

"You're okay," says Michael. "You're okay."

They emerge from the room. He holds her hand like a little kid clutching his mummy in a crowded mall. Stares straight ahead, not at me, which is both a relief and a disappointment. "Here we go," she says. "Here we go, doll."

They vanish around the corner. Only then do I start to relax. Only then do I feel muscles unclenching that I didn't know were tight. Like getting off a roller coaster and only realizing when you are standing on solid ground how terrifying the ride really was.

And what did it accomplish? Was it what I wanted?

I had thought that by seeing Michael's life differently, I'd be able to get her to be my friend but instead I just feel overwhelmed. She's so *perfect* and her life — her family — is so *overly* weird, the contrast is jarring. It's information I feel like I don't know how to process. Like trigonometry. I can see that it should make sense, but it doesn't.

Michael and I have something in common. We have siblings that are "not well." We have siblings that are not there. Not really. Our siblings have disappeared: mine literally, and hers metaphorically. Present but not here. Absent but there.

Suddenly, I *miss* the other Yale so intensely it feels like a pain travelling down my body in a collapsing wave. How can you miss someone you have never met?

I stand there for a while. I stare into Michael's brother's empty bedroom. Sully. Yale never had a bedroom, at least not in the house where I live. Unless my bedroom was her bedroom. Did they give her away right away, or did they wait?

It's completely dark outside now and the moon is perfectly framed by the red curtains hanging down over the window, partially open. What time is it? They eat late.

I forget to feel like an intruder. Whatever fear I had is gone. Michael's family shots all look awkward and posed. In the pictures, Michael is always as distant from the rest of the group as her brother. She looks detached, not like *part* of them. I feel almost sorry for her. She looks alone.

She looks *lonely*. Her sisters are always touching. Her mother wears terrible glasses. Her father has an unusual nose. Her brother always off to the side, staring. He is so good-looking. Really good-looking. Heart-stoppingly good-looking.

I stare for longer than I should before I start to feel awkward in my own skin. Ill-fitting. Like I can't hold the fade any longer. Then, out of nowhere, comes the sick, guilty feeling, like I've done something awful. Like it's a violation of Michael's family for me to have seen that they went to the Grand Canyon a dozen years ago. Worse, I have a strong desire to take one of the pictures. Just to take it.

I feel guilty for wanting it.

I couldn't do it.

I reach out. I touch one of the frames and it disappears. There is a white patch on the wall. I quickly let go.

The heat is getting to me, the strange burning feeling. Making it hard to think and to focus.

I can only stay vanished for ten minutes at a time before it starts to feel terrible. It starts to feel wrong. Painful. Too much. Like every nerve ending is jangling, every nerve experiencing the noise and vibration of a dentist's drill.

I hurry back down the stairs, not caring anymore if someone sees me. Knowing I have to get out of there. It's like when I'm on a bus, sometimes I get overcome by panic. I have to leave. I have to escape. Escape, escape, escape.

I burst out through the front door, leaving it open behind me. I run, flat out sprint, barefoot. My boots in my hand. My feet feeling every bump on the ground, every knob of chewed gum. Every pebble and shard of broken glass. Until finally, I'm blocks away, my breath coming in sharp gasps. My legs hurting and cramping. Then, and only then, do I allow myself to reappear, hunched over, struggling for breath.

No one sees.

No one is there. The darkness is my cloak, hiding me even when I'm not gone.

I feel physically terrible. And mentally overwhelmed by guilt. Like I've stolen something I can't give back. I hate that.

I hate myself.

Yet somehow I know I'm going to do it again.

Crazy.

TONY

8

ISRAEL ARRIVES LOUDLY. Like most things he does, I guess. The sound of his skateboard rattling over the broken up pavement is jarring. Rude.

He skates to a halt right in front of me.

"Dude," he says.

Waves the spliff in front of me in a way that he never does, like a PSA about peer pressure. The smell makes my stomach flip, sick. But I take it. I don't know why. I guess I can't think of a good enough reason why not. "I don't like it" doesn't seem like it would fly. I fake a drag — my mouth instantly dry in a way that no amount of water can fix — and shove it back to him. I work up some faint idea of saliva, spit on the ground. His expression is lost in the thin sweet haze of smoke.

"Fuck off," I tell him. Not that nicely. I have a sudden urge to punch him, like my fantasy about beating Joe. He's so Joe-*like*, somehow, so into himself he barely seems to register that I'm not just an extension of him. He doesn't really get that I'm not his possession somehow.

Like I was Joe's brother first, and myself second. Now I'm Israel's best friend and nothing more than that. Nothing separate, not to him.

But I am. I mean, come on. I can choose *not* to be his best friend. Doesn't he get that? I'm not just someone he can push around and make choices for. I'm so angry about this all of a sudden, I feel like I can't contain it. It doesn't make sense, but there it is. I can picture his eye swelling up, his nose bursting into bloom with blood. I can feel my fist making contact in a way that is so visceral that I back up, just in case. I couldn't do that. I mean, on some level, I owe him. He picked up the pieces after Joe. Well, after that whole thing.

His face is too close to mine and somehow, suddenly, *he's* the one who looks menacing. *He's* the one who looks like he has a punch to throw. I haven't got the faintest fucking idea what's with him. I thought it was me that was mad, but apparently not.

I bounce the ball a few times. I feel strange, uneasy. Maybe it's the pot, but not after one puff. Probably not.

He holds his smoke in and shoots it out at me in a straight line. Right at my mouth, like some kind of evil kiss. I wave my hand to clear the air. Is *usually* respects me.

"It's not such a big deal," he says. "Don't be such a freakin' whiny *baby*. This is my *dad's*. You know, he hides it in the toilet tank, like he's going to be busted by the cops at any moment? What a tool."

He laughs. Hard.

I shrug. "So? Thought we were going to do some one-on-one."

I spin the ball on my fingertip. Dribble. The bounce of the ball on the concrete is reassuring. Familiar. The skin of the ball easier to me than my own flesh. The taste of the joint cluttering up my mouth like day-old puke. Awful. I try to spit again but my mouth is like the Sahara.

"Don't feel like it," he says. "Too much sports today. I had hockey this morning. Worked out at lunch. Feeling worn out, you know?"

He stretches like a wild cat. King of the jungle.

"So?" I say. "I worked out, too. And I rowed. Fell in, too."

It's true. I flash back to the morning. Predawn. Still dark on the water, the surface rippled with sticks and trash. The air so cold it makes it all feel so real, so serious.

Now it's warm. I roll up my sleeve and show Is the bruise on my forearm that I got from clumsily climbing back into the boat. It's hard to get back into those tiny sculls. They're as likely as not to flip again when you hoist yourself up if your balance is off even just slightly. And these days, my balance always is. It's like I'm dizzy inside in a way that I can't pinpoint.

Vertigo.

The water was so cold. Dark green. It absorbed me at first. I felt like I had vanished altogether. It was thick like soup. Quicksand. I was disoriented. For a second, my head was under and I opened my eyes and it was so opaque, I thought I was stuck. I thought it was over. The water seemed alive, like it was holding me down. It scared me and I'm *not* scared of water. Please. I learned to swim when I was two. I've been rowing forever.

Yet, for a second, I almost prayed. Even though I stopped believing in shit like God a long time ago.

I shudder. Throw the ball to no one and run after it, playing catch up with it when it rolls. I dribble back.

Shoot at the hoop in the distance.

Israel sits down. Gets up again. Sits down. He's restless. Dangerous.

He looks at me. Hard. "Can't believe you fell in," he said. "I thought only beginners did that. Not you. Thought you were some kind of rowing *star*."

I shrug in response. Bounce the ball off my knee. Wait for him to get going.

He lies all the way back on the ground, his bare arms crossed over his chest. A pile of broken glass glints near his bare legs, but I don't say anything. It's warm yet too cold to be outside in a sleeveless shirt and shorts unless you're working out. He must be cold, not moving. Eyes closed. I feel like saying, "Get a coat on!" but that would make it official: I've turned into my mother. Someone's mother. I ignore him. He's not my job.

No one is my job.

I shiver. Jog back and forth a bit. Stretch.

I never got warm again after that swim, to tell you the truth. The cold water filling up my eyes and ears. *Shake it off*, I tell myself. I bounce up and down to keep my muscles warm. Do a couple of laps around the court, my breath banging out and feet slapping the ground. I feel so noisy I can't stand it. I freeze, stand in place and shoot so my rebound bounces right back at my feet. Bam, bam, bam.

"You're hyper," Is observes from his bed at midcourt. He's almost shouting, but not quite. "Don't you ever *stop*? Man."

"Yeah," I say. I stop.

I throw the ball at him. Two long bounces and it hits his stomach. He throws it back. Far. Hard. Farther than I would have thought he could get it from the ground. I shouldn't underestimate his strength. I scramble for it before it hits the tangle of brambles.

"Tell me what's up with you and Michael," he shouts.

"Nothing," I say, retrieving the ball. I sink five in a row from the foul line. Six. Seven. Eight. Miss.

"She's a tighty," he observes.

"Don't say that," I say. "You sound like a jerk."

"Yeah?" he says. "So? I saw you yesterday. You think you're invisible or something?"

"No," I say. "What do you care? Nothing happened."

"Mmm," he says, making kissing gestures. Licking his arm. "I told Stasia," he says. "She's all jealous."

"Yeah?" I say.

I pretend not to care. I care. I guess I wish I didn't.

"So tell me," he says. "What's happening with Michael? Are you locked in now? What's the story?"

"Nothing," I say. "I don't know."

The truth is that she's so *desperate* up close. It's all over her, her want. It's hard to not just hold onto her. But it feels wrong, like I'm playing a part that isn't mine to play. Like I'm the freaking understudy or something, just subbing for someone else, someone who deserves her more than I do. Who wants her more than I do. She's so *pretty*. But. I don't know, it's just weird. I don't feel … that's it, I guess. I don't feel. Yesterday was such a strange day. Everything felt weird, telescoped, like through a camera lens. And she's right there, pressing up against me. Her lips are incredible. Like, well. I don't know. Somehow it still feels like my duty.

She's a hottie. She totally is. I get that. Everyone wants to get with her, I know it. I know I'm lucky. I've noticed her, sure. I've thought about it, and she doesn't gross me out or anything. But the fact that she likes me always made me feel weird, like I'd somehow be taking advantage of her.

She's one of the prettiest girls in school if you like that sort of thing. And yeah, who doesn't?

She's so *skinny*, though. When I held her, it was like holding onto a baby sparrow or some shit like that, and not in a good way. Bones protruding into me like they were reaching out to spear my skin.

Thin is popular. Everyone is thin. Every girl wants to be, that's for sure. Nothing wrong with it. I should call her tonight. Hook up on the weekend. Do something old-fashioned like offer to take her to a movie or something. She likes me. A lot. I like her okay. Just because the balance is off doesn't make it *all* wrong.

Does it?

I don't say any of that out loud. Instead, I pass the ball to no one, run for it. This time, I catch it before it hits the ground rolling. My right shoulder is sore. Tired or strained, I can't tell which.

Michael's not as *something* as Stasia. I don't have the word. I can't help comparing. They're both great. But Stasia's off-limits, so I shouldn't waste my time even thinking about her. Her dark eyes. Her incredible body.

I'm just thinking too much, that's all. I should just go with it. Enjoy it. Who wouldn't? Michael is hot. That should be all there is to it.

I do a few jump shots. My feet hurt as they slam down on the cold ground. I don't care. Cold sweat spraying off my face.

Stasia is hotter.

"I'll have her if you don't want her," says Israel.

His eyes are closed. I thought he'd gone to sleep. Almost forgot he was there. For a second, I'm confused. Stasia? No, no. Michael. He means Michael.

Israel can get anyone he wants. I'm sure he could have her if he wanted her. I squint at him. He's got four or five girls on the hook, doesn't need more. I couldn't even say who they are, he changes his mind so fast. Quicksilver, like it says on the bottom of his skateboard. He's dozily twirling the wheels with his hands while he lies there. I think about ball bearings. I can hear them spinning.

"I should tell you," he says. "My parents are splitting up."

At first I don't think I hear him right. Maybe he said, "My parents have split the cup." No, that doesn't make sense.

Splitting up.

They can't split up. I don't know why I care, but I do. I pretend I didn't hear him and I start again at one. Two. Three. Something inside me feels like it's cleaving apart. Why? They aren't my parents. My parents are as good as apart already. I don't care.

"Did you hear me?" he yells.

"Yeah," I say. "Sorry, man. I'm …"

"It's okay," he says. "You know, I've gotta go."

He jumps up faster than I would have thought he'd be able to. Jogs a few steps, then drops his board, and he's off down the street, jacket flapping open. Turns into Matti's driveway; his is the first house in sight of this dump. Disappears around the back.

I feel like a jerk.

I'm going to call Michael. She actually would probably understand why I care, even though I don't want to care.

She seems like someone who would get things about loyalty. Family.

Is loyalty important when you're a high school senior? Even the word sounds dumb when I think it out loud.

Eight, nine, ten.

On the way home, I'm going to grab some job applications from the mall. I'll need to get a job probably, in case I don't get a scholarship. Some kind of job just in case Mum doesn't get it together. I asked her this morning about work and she just looked at me; her eyes were so blank it was almost scary. Then, a bit later, I heard her singing in the shower.

She hasn't sung for a long time. She used to always be singing these stupid Broadway songs. She'd never seen any of the shows and I don't know how she knew them all so well, but she'd belt them out. She has a pretty bad singing voice, but she didn't care.

Singing in the shower is huge.

So maybe she'll be okay.

Maybe not.

Why can't it be easier?

For some stupid reason, I feel like crying. For Israel. For my mum. For *me*.

Israel's parents, well, it sounds dumb but I guess they were sort of the dream. Well, fuck it. They were too-good-to-be-true, after all. I should have known. Nothing good lasts, right? You don't have to be brilliant to get that concept.

Anyway, what do I care? *Why* do I care?

I guess families just suck. They all must start out sort of happy, but then it's like a long trip down the toilet. All that emotion swirling around for years until it all ends up in the sewer. Poetic, huh?

I dribble the ball up and down the court. Back and forth. The ball hitting my hand so hard it's like being slapped.

For some reason, I start thinking about when I was a kid, like maybe seven or eight. Me and Joe, we got it in our heads that we had to — *had to* — go to Disneyland. We begged and begged. It looked so perfect on TV. All those happy kids. Sunshine. Mouse ears. The ads sent us into a kind of psychotic bliss. Please, please, please. I was thrilled when they finally said we could go. Those rides! The lights and colours and all that goddamn happiness! Then when we were there, it all fell apart. Joe got caught trying to steal a keychain from a kiosk. Dad lost his temper and shouted at Mum in the ticket line. She had a migraine. It rained so hard that the rain bounced back up from the hot dry ground. I had bad stomach cramps, but I didn't want to tell anyone and then ended up having diarrhea in the bathroom behind the Pirates of the Caribbean ride. The lineups were killer. When we finally got to the front of the first line, Joe wouldn't go on with me because he said I was a baby. So Mum and I went one way, Joe and Dad went another way. So much for happy families. The mouse ears were too expensive. Worse, the rides made me sick and dizzy. Turned out I had an ear infection, a fever, some kind of flu. But, you know what I mean? Disneyland looked so great. But really, it just made me throw up.

An owl out of nowhere hoots loudly, swoops low in front of me. So close I can see the pattern on its feathers. I saw a show once that said that owls are the only birds that fly without any sound at all. Totally silent. Like stealth birds. I believe it. This one, other than the hooting, is quiet as death. I shudder. Drop the ball and it rolls, I jog to pick it up. Through the falling-down fence in the distance, I see a girl approaching and then running by, wearing a long, flapping winter coat. She's moving fast. So fast. In a flat-out sprint. Somehow she looks like that owl, all that brown, like feathers. Her hair, too, lifting in the wind. Her coat looks tattered but it's not. It's just the way it's moving. She's running hard; her feet are pounding the ground. Like she's being chased, but when I look behind her, I can't see anyone. She doesn't seem to see me. She's running with her head down.

I see that it's Yale. Messy hair. Wild eyes, which I glimpse for only a second. Is she crying? Glass necklace bouncing up into her face, she reaches up and grabs it with her hand to stop it from moving.

She doesn't see me.

I feel a pull of attraction to her that I think I've never felt before. Not actually for anyone. And when I say a "pull," I mean it's like a punch in the gut. What is that about? I can't breathe.

It's not that she's pretty. It's not like that. Michael and Stasia are pretty. It's like suddenly I just fall. My stomach drops.

I dribble the ball.

I shoot some more baskets even though I'm just freezing. My heart's beating hard, like maybe I've got that heart disease, that cardiac weakness, that causes athletes to suddenly drop dead on the playing field.

Am I going to drop dead?

My sweat is cold. Ice.

One, two, three. Ten more and then I'll get going. Ten more and I'll head home before it's completely dark.

Michael

9

Angene and Chelsea are making dinner, an exercise that for them involves adding too many foul-smelling vegetables to a pan of sizzling oil and shouting as much as possible. Michael can smell it from her room. The smell seeping into everything. Into her pores, it feels like. If she actually eats it, she'll stink for days. Gross. Garlic and mung beans. She'll make something else, she decides. A salad. Clean fresh vegetables, unfried. Baked chicken. Something okay. She'll make some for Sully, too. He'd never say (well, obviously) but he doesn't like the sisters' choices either. She can tell. Probably it also drives him crazy the way they eat like animals, the grinding of their jaws chewing and the saliva sounds of swallowing. Thinking about it makes her feel sick. She'll take Sully into the den and they'll eat in front of the TV. No one will mind. They think it's "sweet" how she dotes on Sully. She thinks that's patronizing. She doesn't "dote" on him. He's her brother. She takes care of him. Which is more than she can say for the rest of the family. Her dad hiding in his beer can, fixated on the animals. Her mother so consumed by whatever project she's working on (or that the sisters are working on) that she scarcely seems to notice Sully. Or Michael, for that matter.

It's not fair. But what is?

Michael drops down onto her yoga mat without bothering with the cute clothes bought expressly for the purpose. Her clothes don't need to breathe. She just needs to think. To really *think*.

The problem is that Tony hasn't called. She can't even try to meditate because all she is doing is obsessing. From the mat, she reaches for her cell phone and dials up Aurelia to talk about it. Or to try to get a word in edgewise. Two words in and Aurelia has already cut her off with a long gossipy story about Sam hooking up with some guy named Mitch from the track team, something about how he had bad skin and wasn't it gross that Sam would make out with him? And she wasn't even drunk.

"But," Michael wants to say, "I want to talk about Tony." But she doesn't. She realizes right then and there, the phone curled in her hand like a weapon, that her "friend" isn't listening. In fact, never really listens at all.

The stabs of loneliness that Michael has felt lately give her physical pains so intense that she nearly doubles over from them. She can hardly stand the gossipy chatter. The who-said-what-to-who and why The Girls must now hate this person or that. It's just not sitting right with her. She's starting to feel like The Girls are almost — and it's hard to define exactly — but sort of using Michael because she's pretty, a bit like an accessory almost, to decorate the group. It's starting to make her wonder if she really is the "leader," or if that's just something she imagined. It's making her contemplate whether she really even cares.

It's obvious, in fact, that The Girls — Aurelia in particular — are not actually liked. They're just scarily, relentlessly bitchy. Is she, Michael, like that? Is she a bitch, too?

Aurelia is still talking. Hasn't she noticed that Michael isn't responding? She is saying something breathlessly, something she must think is important. Michael listens. The Girls have a new "thing." A mission: getting rid of Yale. Getting her off the gymnastics team. She screwed up, so she's out. Not that she was ever really *in* with The Girls, but she was always around. She wasn't so blatantly outcast. It's like that show on TV, *Survivor*. They want to vote Yale off the island.

"We'll all do it together," Aurelia says confidently. "She won't even know what hit her."

It makes Michael feel tired. "Oh," she says.

So incredibly, heavily tired that she lies down on the mat. After all, what did Yale really do that was so wrong? She must be humiliated beyond anything imaginable. She must die a bit inside every time someone brings it up *again*. All the jokes and the never-let-it-drop mentality are starting, frankly, to embarrass Michael a bit by association.

She's having a really hard time hating Yale for something that's nothing to do with her, having a hard time even listening to Aurelia or Sam or Madison rambling on and on about it. She does not want to talk about how Yale got her period anymore.

She wants to — needs to — focus on herself, if she's being honest. She'd rather Aurelia and Sam and Madison came over to have a break-it-down conversation about

Tony, about what she must be doing wrong. Really, she just wants — needs! — their reassurance that it's not her, it's him. There's something wrong with *him*.

Not her.

She must have PMS or something because she feels over-whelmed. Weepy. Even feels a bit like crying right now, listening to Aurelia spill the details of the "plan."

"I have to go," she says. Michael hangs up the phone, sits up straight on her mat, concentrates on her medita-tion. Hope has told her that she's doing well with it, although Michael has no idea how she would know. Maybe that's why, lately, she has felt like she's being watched. Maybe Hope has installed some kind of camera in her room, to make sure she's really doing her therapy homework. To make sure she's really breathing.

Well, she's not. The joke's on Hope. Meditating is just time for her to obsess. When she closes her eyes, she can easily see a visual compilation of all her flaws. For example, she's getting a cold sore. Gross. She probably gave it to Tony. She knows that cold sores are herpes, so she gave him herpes. Great. He'll love that.

No wonder he didn't call.

The phone rings and rings. Sam. Aurelia. Madison. Again. She doesn't pick up. Can't stand any of them, not right now. Not when she feels this way.

The jeans she wore today were too tight. All day she was aware of the small fold of her belly sticking out over the top. She was so anxious about it she literally felt like her head was going to explode if she didn't change, but there was no way to come home and do that. Besides which, her punishment for being such a fat pig *should* be to wear gross, uncomfortable, ugly jeans that make her look terrible. Her hair is a disaster; split ends are waving around the top of her skull like tiny antennae.

"Breathe," she reminds herself, out loud, forcefully. She can hear Sully smashing around in his closet. What is he doing in there? Should she go check?

Her sisters are nearby though. If he were in trouble, they'd hear. She needs this time to meditate. She can hear Angene singing in the hallway. There, she's taking care of it. Maybe. Hopefully. The song stops. There's the sound of someone mock tap dancing. Well.

She shudders at the reminder of how weird her sister is. But at the same time, she's glad her sisters live here sometimes. Like now, for example, when Mum and Dad are away at some kind of horrifying animal-stuffing convention in Boise. The idea of being alone in the house gives her nightmares. When it does happen, which hasn't been very often, she lies awake all night. Eyes glued open by her completely crazy and irrational belief that the animals' ghosts will come for her. Animal zombies, risen from the dead.

"Too many of those stupid movies," she says out loud.

"Talking to myself," she adds.

Somehow saying it out loud makes her feel worse, so she stops.

"Breathe," she says again. "Breathe." She concentrates on the in and out. In (garlic and mung bean grossness fills her nose). Out (she feels her exhalation on her cold sore and it stings).

Tears fill her eyes. She stares at the phone. *Ring, goddamn you*, she thinks.

Angene — or maybe it's Chelsea, their voices are impossible to tell apart — shouts at her for dinner.

Everyone is always shouting, she thinks. *This house is too big.*

She shouts back, almost drowning out the ringing phone. She picks it up.

"Hello?"

"Michael?"

"Yes?"

"It's me."

"Tony?"

She's confused. The call display shows a name she doesn't recognize right away. "Matti?"

He laughs. "No," he says. "It's Is. I'm using Matti's phone."

"Is," she says. Like he calls all the time. "Hey."

"Hey, yourself," he says. "Wondering if you wanted to hook up this weekend."

"Oh," she says. "Sure. I mean, okay."

"Cool," he says. "Bunch of us going up to the lakes."

"Bunch of us?" she says.

"Yeah," he says. "Me and Matti. Jason and his girl. You."

"Oh," she says. "Not Tony?"

"No," he says. "Problem?"

"Oh," she says. She's saying that too much. "No problem. Cool."

She hangs up.

What is that? she thinks. *What is that about?* Israel has never paid much attention to her before. They have the same friends. She was with Matti for about ten seconds last year. So their paths crossed at parties.

Matti was a jackass. He always drank so much. He almost always threw up. Disgusting. His breath always smelled like Doritos. He liked to grab at her chest in a way that made her want to scream at him. Always grappling with her clothes, like they were impossible to remove. Still it was somehow okay. She felt like she was wrapped in cellophane when she was around him. Like she was protected by a barrier that he couldn't penetrate. Mostly because he probably didn't want to. Likely it was all for show. He never ever kissed her, which — now that she thinks about it — was pretty weird. She's almost sure he's gay. Spends more time on his hair than she does and that's saying a lot.

Oh well, she thinks. She looks at herself in the mirror. "You're pretty," she says. She feels prettier somehow. At least someone wants her. Maybe not Tony, but Israel Santiago. Well, everyone wants him.

She's somebody.

Not that she really wants ... well. There's something about Israel that unsettles her. His eyes. The way he moves. The way he always has a girl sticking a tongue in his ear, touching his lap. The way he seems to need that, like it feeds him. Like the girls are clothes he's wearing to look cooler. But more than that, it's like he's sexually overcharged. He's too much.

Especially for her.

Don't be stupid, she tells herself. He's just another boy. Besides, maybe Tony will be jealous. Maybe he'll care. In any event, it's just one weekend. Just for a night. She can keep Israel off her, she's sure of it. And it will sure make Tony wonder. It will make him want her more. She's almost — almost — sure of it.

Yale

10

This class won't end. Maybe ever. Maybe this is going to go on for all of eternity, with the cedar chip smell of the urine-soaked hamster cage making my mouth pucker with nausea. I watch the rodents run through their Habitrail. The stench feels like it's clogging up my brain. Tony isn't here today. Neither is Israel.

Michael has a hickey on her neck. I find my eyes keep sliding over to her, staring at the bruise. I heard that she and Tony hooked up. Is that Tony's hickey? Probably. Who cares?

I do. It makes me feel funny. Nervous, somehow. A bit sick. Michael keeps touching it. Tipping her head to the side. Smiling, texting back and forth with Samantha, obviously, both of them alternating typing and laughing. Flicking their hair. That way that they have gets to me, that "Look at us, we're *such* good friends; everything is funny to us because we're protected by the bubble of each other." The smugness.

If I were being honest, I guess I'd say I was jealous.

Michael's hand reaches up again. Rubs the mark. Okay, okay, we get it. You have a hickey. Big deal. Her fingers feather her neck again. Highlighting, pointing, showing off. I force myself to look away. Concentrate on twirling my pen between my thumb and forefinger. My cuticle is raw and sore.

Mr. Eggerton is handing back our papers. He holds each one up before returning it, inspecting it in the light as though it's one of those children's stickers that change when you angle them just so. It's taking forever.

I stretch my legs out under my desk and back again. So taut. My muscles in a constant state of aching from the disappearances. I jog them up and down. Somehow it's a relief to do this, like the jittering of my limbs relieves some of the jittering inside of me.

"Stop fidgeting, Miss Grant," says Mr. Eggerton. He's standing over me. He's so close I can see the ring around the collar of his shirt. Dirt. Sweat. Disgusting.

Still, one thing about Mr. Eggerton is that no matter how strange he is, he has kind eyes. I'd never admit to anyone how much I actually like Mr. Eggerton because of this. "If you need to visit the bathroom," he says, "please go."

"Need a tampon?" someone says from the back of the room. A girl. Who was it? I swing my head around to see, fast enough to blur the laughing faces. Everyone thinks it's hilarious.

It's always hilarious when it isn't you, I guess.

That particular embarrassment probably won't end. I concentrate on Mr. Eggerton's eyes so I don't accidentally fade. I'm getting so that doesn't happen. Not now. Not from embarrassment. Not accidentally. I have more control now. I'm figuring it out. I'm figuring out a lot of things. Like Michael. Not like we're friends or anything, but somehow ...

This morning, I bumped into her in the bathroom. She was frowning at herself in the mirror and I could almost hear her voice saying, "Fat pig." So I said, "Those jeans make you look so thin, you're so lucky." Big deal, right? Wasn't hard for me to say. But she lit up. She did. She smiled at me like she genuinely liked me.

"Your paper," Mr. Eggerton says. It kind of floats toward me, jars me back into the room.

"Tampon, tampon, tampon," someone chants.

"Quiet," snaps Mr. Eggerton. "One more idiotic comment and everyone gets detention." He gives me a sympathetic look.

I blush hard. My eyes are watering. Why do I let them get to me? I hold my paper in my hands like it's the most interesting thing in the world.

I got an F. I can't believe it. Quickly, I flip the paper over so no one sees it. I feel sick, like I'm actually going to have a heart attack. I've never got an F on anything before. Suddenly, I can imagine myself flunking grade twelve. Having to stay an extra year. No future. Another year of maxi-pads stuck to my locker door.

Another year of humiliation.

I swallow hard so I don't cry. I know it's extreme. I'm overreacting. It's just a paper. Who cares?

Mr. Eggerton has moved on. "Miss Hyde-Smith," he says. "Terrible work, as usual." There's more laughter. I smile, too. Fake a laugh. It feels like I'm choking on a wasp.

"Ha dee ha," says Michael. "You're funny, Mr. E."

"It's Eggerton," he says.

"Okay, Eggerton," she says.

"Miss Hyde-Smith," he says, like he's going to get mad. But then he laughs. Laughs? She's flirting. I feel wronged. His laugh sounds underused, rusty.

Everyone loves Michael.

It's not fair. *Miss Hyde-Smith*. Even her name sounds better than everyone else's.

In big red letters on the back page of my essay — I can see through the paper — it says, SEE ME. Why does it have to be in block letters? Is it that serious?

I can't remember writing this paper. Above the SEE ME, I can see words that I must have typed.

My hand is shaking. Well, that's normal.

I start to draw on the paper, to steady it. I sketch Michael, quickly. Then Aurelia and Sam. Sort of caricatures, I guess. Like they're lollipops. Soon I can't see the writing through the whiteness anymore. I concentrate on the drawing. There's more laughter, I don't hear what's funny. As long as it's not about me, I don't care.

I have a crazy urge to follow Mr. Eggerton home tonight. See where he lives. Spy on him in the bathroom or something equally twisted. Maybe I should start taking pictures or something. Blackmail. I can make him change my grade.

No, no, no.

That isn't me.

That would *definitely* be wrong.

I won't go that far. I know it as clearly as I can smell the hot lamp of the overhead projector, the smell of the erasable markers that Mr. Eggerton uses, the mixed smells of soap, perfume and Lysol that backfill every classroom.

I am not evil.

Someone taps me on the shoulder. Michael.

"I got an F, too," she says conspiratorially.

"Oh," I say. I can't read her expression. It's either bitchy or friendly. Vindictive or shy. "Too bad."

But my tone is all wrong. It comes out sarcastic. Harsh. Mean. I don't know why that happens. Why do I do that? Her face closes up, just like that, like a sea anenome closing over a crab.

"I mean, that sucks," I add lamely, but it's too late, she's already turned away again, her hair sleekly falling toward me like a blade. I back away so it doesn't touch me. Suddenly it looks dangerous.

I almost say, "Breathe," but I don't.

The bell rings, loudly. So loudly that I jump. Stuff my paper into my backpack. Head for the door.

"Miss Grant," says Mr. Eggerton, in front of me suddenly. "See me, please."

"Practice," I mumble, pushing past him. "Gymnastics, can't be late." It's not a lie. It's Monday, gymnastics right after school Monday, Wednesday, Thursday. It's true that I've missed practice before but in this school, sports rules everything. "Practice" can get you out of anything.

He's so close that I can smell his Tic Tacs, orange flavour. Smell his shampoo, it smells like tar, some kind of dandruff stuff I guess. A haze of body odour and sweat, cheap deodorant with some kind of harsh metallic tang. "Tomorrow, then," he says. For a second, it seems like he's going to actually put his hand on my shoulder. I flinch. Someone pushes past me from behind.

"Sorry," Aurelia says. She always spits when she talks. Her breath smells like roasted chicken. "You're kind of like standing right in the door."

"I know," I say. "I was just …" but she's gone.

My arms and legs feel heavy. Anika smiles at me as I go past her locker, but it seems too hard to smile back. Down the end of the hall, I see Tony and Israel in a huddle by the water fountain. Nice of them to show up for class. For irrational reasons, I feel like shouting at them. Tony glances up at me, and I swear that he winces. I glower at him for good measure. So what if his skin smells good? Who cares? I don't need him. I don't have a crush.

I don't.

I don't need anyone. I don't need for him to like me back. I just like him because of the singing. Because he was so sad. He had a brother who died, you know? So maybe I just like him because he would understand about the absence, I think. I think he would get how much I miss the other Yale, even though I've never even seen a picture of her.

There's a knot in my stomach like hunger or sickness. I chew a piece of strong mint gum that I can taste in my nose as I exhale. It burns. I can't miss practice. Today we're setting our routines for the next meet, the nationals. It's important.

Is it?

Suddenly it doesn't feel important.

I feel almost like turning left, going down the stairs and running out into the rain. It's pouring — spring rain saturating everything, warm water hitting the ground like a shower and the scent of everything green bouncing back in the cleansed air. I can almost feel the water on my skin.

Smell how fresh it must be, the water so thick coming from the sky that all the foul odours are temporarily tamped down, muffled under the rest.

There aren't nearly enough windows in this school, but through the funny narrow slits cut high in the walls near the ceiling, I can see nothing but water, water, more water.

The school is sinking.

I wish. I take a deep breath, mostly of sweat and musty books and hair products, all overwritten by the ubiquitous smell of Lysol. I don't have time for fresh air.

I trudge on through the seething halls to the gym. The volume is incredible now that school is over for the day. It's like people are exploding out of themselves to escape. I wonder if everyone hates it here as much as I do.

Maybe I'm not so unique, after all. If I spied on everyone here, would I see that everyone is just as freaked out as me?

I don't want to believe that. I want to think everyone is happy. Everyone. Even the people I don't like. Even the people I don't know.

Someone trips in front of me, dropping a math book on my foot. I keep going. All over the place cell phones are ringing and beeping and playing songs. Kids are listening to iPods, hunching over, acting invisible. Some are hugging each other, shouting, dancing.

Idiots, I think. I feel more comfortable hating them for their entitlement; I don't want to feel sorry for them for covering up.

The Girls are already in the change room when I get there. Laughing loudly in that obnoxious way that makes me lonely.

Aurelia is pretending to kiss Madison, a scene that

would send most boys in the school into some kind of orgasmic hysteria. They're shrieking with laughter in a way that suggests that kissing girls is somehow gross, yet also risqué and daring and sexy.

I avoid Michael's eyes and more specifically her neck. She's looking at it in the mirror, her thin neck rising like a reed out of her perfectly matching Lululemon outfit that probably cost two hundred and fifty dollars. "Does this show a lot?" she says to me, through the mirror.

I pretend I don't know what she's talking about. "What?" I say.

"This," she says, frowning at her neck. She touches it again, like she can brush it off.

"Yeah," I say. "It shows."

For a second she looks upset, and I wish I'd said more, but I can't think of anything else. There's a pause, and then she expertly fills it by laughing. "Oh, well," she says. "Too bad." Her laugh doesn't reach her eyes, though. I can see that.

Samantha makes a kissing noise, and they all start laughing again. Too hard. Michael's laughing, too, but she isn't happy. Or maybe I just think that because, now that I've stolen a look into her house, I feel like I know her. Like feeling that you know a celebrity just because you've seen a few films that they're in.

I change quickly, my back to them, stuffing my things into my locker. Noticing that someone has stuck instructions from a box of tampons onto the door. Funny. Sam looks at me and smirks, showing a flash of braces. For a second, I'm furious. Why does she think she's so great? She isn't pretty, not really. She has people fooled into thinking that she is but that has more to do with expensive clothes. A good haircut. A lot of makeup. I mean, give me a *break*. She has braces years after everyone else got them off. Why does *she* get to laugh at *me*? I snarl. Out loud. Like one of those yappy, filthy dogs. Close the door to the locker hard with a shuddering bang, drop the HOW TO INSERT paper on the ground.

Michael, washing her hands, moves slightly to let me past. Aurelia calls my name and I stop and turn. "You forgot these," she says, sweetly but not sweetly, holding out the box of tampons that the instructions came from.

So funny.

"Ha dee ha," I hiss. I feel almost feral. Like I could turn into an animal of some sort and just out and out attack.

I force myself to move past Michael and the sink. The soap smells like something medicinal, not like you would expect soap to smell. She's intent on the washing. She doesn't look up.

"Hurry," I say. "We'll be late."

Then she catches my eye. "I'm hurrying," she says. "Go ahead."

"I'm going," I say. I run into the gym, sidling past Madison, who refuses to move or meet my eye. What is going on? What are they up to?

Something. I can feel it on my skin. My heart thumps irregularly.

It's cold in the gym. I jog on the spot, to stay warm. My T-shirt has a hole in it exactly over my belly button. It makes both the hole in the shirt and my navel look ridiculous, endless, comical. I stick my finger in it and pull, the threads tight on my skin. My shirt says BOULDER, COLORADO over a picture of a horse and a setting sun. I've never been to Boulder.

Coach clears her throat. (She's always doing that, like a big cat who's licked herself too much, swallowed too much hair.) "Okay," she says. "Okay." Her voice is hushed, but also loud. Coach is one of those women who look like a man trying to be a woman. *Sexually ambiguous* is how I would phrase it. Or *asexual*. Her asexuality makes me feel bad. It makes me feel too girly. It makes me feel silly.

Dumb.

She shifts back and forth from one foot to the other. She has huge feet. She must wear men's shoes. I'd never noticed before. Her shoes are new and glowing white. "Okay," she says again.

The gym always feels so big at this time of day, the equipment set up over at the far end, no one else around. Sometimes the whole school is crammed in here for pep rallies and other wastes-of-time. Now with just five of us — six now that Michael runs in, her long ponytail bouncing from side to side — it feels hollow. Like we're on the inside of an echo.

"Okay," says Samantha impatiently. Bitchily.

Coach clears her throat. (See: hairball.)

"Coach, what are you trying to say?" Samantha has a way of talking to everyone like they work for her, which sadly usually works to make them answer her respectfully.

"I have here," Coach says, waving her clipboard, "the events for the meet on April third. I've decided to enter you in these events. Um, let's see." She squints at her own writing, and then starts listing. I tune her out until she gets to me. "Yale," she says. "Beam and floor."

"Beam and floor," I repeat.

"Beam and floor," she says.

"But," I say. "What about bars? Bars are my best event. We need for me to do it. I mean, I'll get the most points."

"Oh, no," she says.

Samantha rolls her eyes. "Obviously you don't want to do those again," she says. "Duh. Well, *we* wouldn't want you to, anyway. Isn't that right, Coach?"

Aurelia chortles as though that was the funniest thing she ever heard. Coach looks slightly abashed. Or at least I think she does. She clears her throat again. "Well," she says. "Well. The thing is that what happened to you last time, well. It was just embarrassing. For the team. The whole team. The school. For their sake, you won't do bars again."

"What?" I say. I press my fingers against the bruise on my forehead. "What?"

"C'mon, Tampax," says Samantha in a singsong voice. "Think about it."

"I assumed you'd understand," Coach starts. "Girls …" she pleads. Her obsequiousness with The Girls makes me want to scream. She *kowtows* to them. She's like the fat kid in junior high school who would do anything to be liked. Suddenly, I get a flash of Coach as a teenager. Coach on the outskirts of groups like The Girls. Coach dying to be liked.

Well, *fuck* her. She's adult now. I stare at her mouth, moving. I can't hear her. There's a roar in my ears like a million crows cawing at once. I swear, I feel wings against my skin.

I turn, my shoes squeaking.

I force one foot after the other. Concentrate on walking fast but not too fast. Someone could stop me if they tried.

They don't try.

I'm walking away from the only thing about this horrible place that I like. I want them to stop me, and I don't. I'm leaving. I guess I'm gone.

Wearing my gym clothes still, I walk out of the gym through the emergency exit. An alarm rings, a loud beep reverberates behind me, within me, bells so loud they shake my guts. I keep walking. The rain hits me hard. The gravel is covered with deep puddles. I walk onto the field. It's windier than I had thought. The grass is soaking and muddy. I start to run toward my scooter, but then I realize my keys are inside my locker.

I disappear. It's the first time I've done it out of anger. It's like they can go fuck themselves if they think they'll see me again. "Never," I'm saying out loud. "Never." I'm so hot, I'm burning. The taste of pennies and kerosene is strong in my mouth. I feel faint. If I faint when I'm faded, will I ever come back?

I go back to get my keys, I have to. I go through the front door, back to the change room. It seems to take forever. No one is around. The empty halls are filthy from muddy feet. In the math room the janitor doesn't look up from his slow-motion wiping of the chalkboard.

I'm dripping water like crazy — what kind of rain is that? It's a monsoon, a typhoon, the apocalypse — which I notice only in the deserted halls. The change room reverberates with emptiness, but I can hear The Girls' voices rising and falling in the gym. I feel disoriented. Dizzy. Scared.

I get my stuff. Grab my keys. Practice rings on without me. The thud of someone jumping off the beam. The thwap, thwap, thwap of someone doing a tumbling run. The sound of the springboard someone is using to mount the bars or the beam or the horse. The sounds of gymnastics.

Frankly, I don't care if I never hear those sounds again.

I do care.

I don't.

I slip into the gym. My feet slap, slap, slapping the floor. The gym smell saturating everything. Aurelia is on the bars, her body thwapping the lower bar as she prepares to dismount, her body a rubber band. Madison is on the beam, deep in conversation with Coach. Sam and Michael are stretching on the mat, having an intense conversation. I move as close as I dare, protected by the shadows of the banners hanging overhead.

"I just think it isn't necessary," Michael is saying. "Why do you care that much about her? She's good on the team."

Sam smirks. "It worked, didn't it? Now she won't be an issue."

"But that's just stupid," says Michael. "She was the best on the team. Now we'll never win."

Sam looks affronted. "Yeah, but we won't be humiliated either."

"For fuck's sake," snaps Michael. "It was an accident. You are such a bitch."

"What?" says Sam. The air around them seems dangerous. Heated. A vibration of something that's almost a colour.

"You heard me," says Michael coldly. She reaches over to stretch her left leg. I can see her hand is shaking.

"Yeah," says Sam. "I did."

My heart is going crazy. What was that? What just happened?

In my confusion, I almost reappear. I see my own foot and I realize I have to concentrate.

I run. Out through the change room and back down the empty hall so no one sees the door slam behind me. As soon as I'm safely outside, I let myself come back. It's so cold at first. The transition is getting more extreme, it seems. Like a fever so bad you could convulse, eyes rolling back, lips blue. I shiver, bite my tongue.

I walk back to my scooter, shaking.

Well.

That's over.

But what really happened? Michael saying, "You are such a bitch." The way the air crackled around her, the way The Girls seemed to move away in a pack. Was Michael standing up for me? Was she defending *me*?

Because that's what it looked like. That's how it felt.

My scooter judders underneath me, moving over a puddle dangerously, skimming and slipping. I try to concentrate on the road. The cars. People have their headlights on because the storm is making it so dark. The cars coming toward me are blinding me and then in turn choking me with their exhaust. The scooter shakes dangerously. "Don't break down," I whisper. Not today.

I go to Michael's house, telling myself it's because it's closer than mine, but that isn't the true reason. (It's easy to lie to yourself when there is something you want that you know is wrong.) I can't help it, it's like I have to do it now. I have to see *something*. What, I don't know. Something *more*. I park the scooter in the playground across the street, lean it up against a bright yellow plastic slide with water running down it like a river. I wait until I don't think anyone can see me and go up to the door.

It's not locked but it's obvious no one is home. Even in the deafening rain, I can hear that the house is empty. Where is Sully? I wonder. Do they take him out places? Obviously. I mean, of course they do. Does he walk? Does he have a wheelchair? Where do they go? Does he do normal things, like go to movies?

I wonder if the other Yale gets taken out. Who takes her? I hope it's someone who loves her. I hope someone *cares*.

I go in like it's the most natural thing in the world. I walk from room to room, dripping on the carpet, which absorbs the water, rendering it instantly invisible like some kind of scary green sponge. There's nothing new to see that I haven't seen already, not really. The pictures are the same. The closed doors. The dead squirrel on the stair railing. The deer's head peering around the corner. But it sort of feels new. I go into Michael's room — which is new to me — and look in her closet. (How creepy am I? Does this cross the line?) Her clothes are all perfectly arranged by colour. Everything smells like fresh dry cleaning. Each hanger has a small sachet of potpourri that smells like vanilla and something floral. Her shoes are lined up evenly on the floor by colour, and then by heel height.

Everything is perfectly in place. For some reason, this makes me feel sad. I'm about to walk away, when I see the notepad on her bedside table. There are doodles on it. The name "Tony" written over and over. "Israel." And then, under that, "Yale."

What does that mean?

A passing car throws light up against the wall that startles me. It's bright, like a spotlight. It highlights how I shouldn't be here.

What gives me the right to do this? It's all wrong. So why can't I stop?

I make myself leave, closing the door carefully behind me. It's raining harder than ever. Can it rain this hard? There is almost no space between raindrops, just sheets of water falling from the sky like solid objects being dropped.

I'm drenched. Uncomfortable. Cold. But I don't care.

I leave the scooter and walk for a while, completely hidden by the thick falling water. I walk to Tony's house. I can't pretend (even to myself) that it's an accident. I do it completely on purpose. It's creepy and wrong but I've started and now I can't stop.

Just one more time, I tell myself, but already I can tell that I'm lying. My ability to do this is like a narcotic and I'm hooked.

Sick.

I crouch beside a shrub near his front walk. Why? I'm invisible. The front door is partially open, as though a dog has just escaped. I push it and go inside.

Dark. It's so dark, it takes my eyes a second to adjust. I'm leaving wet footprints on the thickly carpeted white stairs. The TV is a flickering light in the room at the end of the hall. I go in. Someone is asleep on the sofa. Must be his mother. Sleeping like a child, curled into fetal position. The other rooms are empty.

I go into a room that I think must be his. Definitely his. It smells like him. I am so attuned to his scent that I think I could probably track him, like a bloodhound. *Like one of those dogs.*

He has posters on the wall of bands that I'd never have guessed he listened to. *I'm such a creep*, I think. But I can't stop looking.

Violating.

It's not like I'm looking at him naked. Not like I'm doing anything wrong. (But it is.) (I am.)

I lie down on his bed. It smells so much like him, I get dizzy. It's too much. Earthy. Fresh. I hang over the edge and peek underneath. Under it, comic books spill out in piles. I grab one. It's full of naked, big boobs.

Oh.

The dizziness changes to something else.

I drop the magazine back on the ground.

That's too much information, I think. It's too personal. I don't want to picture him with this magazine, doing what he's probably doing. I feel funny, bad, in a way I can't identify.

Yes, I can. I feel *embarrassed*.

I'm so flustered that I accidentally reappear, which makes what I'm doing seem even more wrong. *I don't belong here.* I catch sight of myself in Tony's mirror. It takes me a minute to fade again. Long enough that I panic, my breath coming in short bursts. I can't forget how to do it now, I can't.

I force myself to stand up, walk out into the hall, into the next open doorway. This room is unnaturally still. It's … oh. Well, it's obviously his brother's room. There's the musty smell of a room that isn't used. Where no one lately has moved around, breathed. The room of someone dead.

My heart is racing. Poor Tony.

I feel so confused. Strange. My head is spinning.

I go out the same way I came in, but faster. I close the door tight behind me. His mum must be cold in there on the sofa. Seems only fair to protect her a bit from all the rain and cold wetness of outside.

There are three more places where I feel like I have to go.

I start at Aurelia's. I have been there only once before and that was a birthday party when we were so young that all parents automatically invited everyone in the whole class. She's always hated me, I don't know why. I remember in the seventh grade, I got a sweater for Christmas that I'd wanted more than anything. Man, I loved that sweater. It was purple. Puffed sleeves. Awful now that I think about it, but so ideal at the time. I couldn't live without it. I wore it to school the first day back after winter break, wore it feeling pretty for a change, feeling okay. She was wearing the same sweater.

The look of horror on her face was scary.

She came right up to me, slammed me up against a locker — impressive because she's really, really tiny — and said, right into my face, "If you ever wear that again, I'll kill you." She scared me. I threw it out and pretended that I'd lost it. She's like that. There's something in her eyes that says you should be scared. That there's good reason for it.

I don't go in, after all. I just change my mind. I make excuses to myself: there are two cars parked outside, so someone is definitely home. I can hear a dog barking inside and I don't know what a dog would make of me. It sounds big, like a Rottweiler or a pit bull or something else that she probably has trained to attack. She's like that. I'm willing to bet the dog would go for me anyway, an apparition sneaking up the stairs. And I'm willing to bet that Aurelia's dog is as scary as Aurelia.

The truth is that I really don't want to be close to Aurelia's things. I don't want to know anything about her.

I don't want to know her at all.

Next.

Staying gone like this is starting to hurt. There's a feeling in my chest like something trying to get out, something pushing on my flesh. The next house is Samantha's. I know she isn't there, but I go inside. I go straight to her room.

The funny thing is that of all The Girls, Sam and I were the closest to being actual real friends. When we were little kids, we took a ballet class together. I used to come here when we were small. Her mum used to look after me after school sometimes. I can't exactly remember why, but I remember that it stopped when her mum found out that my mum smoked pot. I remember Sam hissing to Aurelia in the cloakroom, "Mum says Yale's mum's a pothead." And the horror in her voice.

But it was a fake friendship, anyway. Do little kids have real friendships? It was forced by circumstance. Still, I used to love it here. Her mum always made butterscotch chip cookies. So good. She was like a storybook mum, always baking and pouring glasses of milk and braiding Sam's hair and making her clothes by hand, which Sam hated.

Sam was okay back then. That was before she became one of The Girls. Before Madison was even at our school. Before Sam turned into someone better than me. Before she started hating me for whatever it is that they hate so much.

Her mum and dad are drinking wine down in the kitchen — I can hear the clink of glass against the marble counter, the glug, glug, glug of it being poured. (Wine seems like such a proper, adult thing to drink, so not like my parents drinking Kool-Aid and smoking dope, that I'm actually jealous.) They're cooking something in the kitchen. I hear chopping and sizzling. It smells incredibly good, garlicky and like frying meat. I'm leaving wet foot-prints everywhere on the shiny wood floors.

Samantha's room is papered over with pictures of models posing, models caught at airports, models on magazine covers, models on catwalks. The girl has a problem, I think. She's five feet tall. Does she imagine this being her own life?

I think, it would be so easy to get her to like me. I think of this morning in the bathroom with Michael. One little compliment. I study the pictures. There are a lot of Gisele Bündchen. I could say, "You know, you look a little like Gisele." It wouldn't be totally untrue. She does, a bit. Maybe. It's a stretch, but it would make her happy. Maybe that's all there is to it, just making them happy.

I sit on her bed, leaving more moisture from the rain. She still has the white ornate dresser and desk set from when she was little. Her walls are still painted pink. A stuffed dog called Snoop is still tucked into her sheets by her pillow.

Weird.

I touch her things but I can't feel them and, as I touch them, they fade away. I hold Snoop in my arms and then put him back. For a minute, I think about looking for a diary but I don't. I don't know Sam now, but I used to. I don't want to stumble on too much. You know? Then I take a scarf. I don't know why. I just take it. It looks like something that would be itchy, purple and green with small jewels knitted into the wool. I'd never wear it. It's ugly. I stuff it into my coat pocket.

I go out the front door, leave it swinging open behind me. I bet the cat will escape. I bet Sam will get blamed.

Last, but not least, I guess: Madison's.

Madison's house is huge. It's comic-book big, like something that isn't real. I bet they have staff.

I stand at the front door, hesitating. What am I looking for? Why did this feel like something I needed to do?

There are alarm stickers all over the glass. Could I trigger an alarm? I'm tired. And I'm too scared to try the heavy wood door. Too scared of getting caught. Her house is so huge and serious and intimidating. It's beautiful, too. No wonder she acts so entitled. Look what she *has*; look where she lives.

I give up without even trying. It feels like I've been faded forever.

I reappear and jog through the rain, which has now faded to a drizzle, like the intensity of the weather (of everything) has just passed. I go back to my scooter. Lights are on in Michael's house now. Cars in the driveway. They're home, then. I'm tempted to look again, see what they are doing. Listen. But I force myself to leave.

I go home.

I feel strange. Buoyed up. All the lights are on. The living room, dining room, kitchen, all the rooms are empty. I start to go into my own room and hesitate. There is one more thing I have to do, to see. I want to see my parents. I want to … I can't explain. Just be with them, I guess, but not have to talk about Yale or anything. I just want to sit with them for a few minutes. That's all. So even though it's making my skin throb in a way that's reminding me to get back to myself, I vanish again.

I'm not home either.

I go downstairs.

I can hear Mum and Dad, typing, typing, typing. The smell of marijuana is everywhere, crawling through the vents, saturating. Overwhelming all the other normal smells. I crouch under the table, glad that they are so ensconced that they wouldn't see me even if they looked. It feels safe to be there, seeing them when they can't see me. I can't explain, but it's what I wanted. For a second I'm reminded of when I was really small, like two or three, and I ran away from my mum in a busy shopping mall. Then I couldn't find her. I ran and ran and finally someone found me, picked me up and called my name — my first name because I didn't know my last — through the PA system. And my mum appeared, completely calm and unharried. In retrospect, she probably hadn't noticed I was gone, but at the time it felt like I was being saved from something so big and scary it couldn't even be mentioned.

"Are you done yet?" says Mum. Her voice startles me.

"No," says Dad. "I'll tell you the second I'm out."

"Are we doing the right thing?" she says.

"It's the last time," he says. "Think of it like we're Robin Hood." He laughs, and then so does she, the strange laugh she gets when she's been smoking — giggly, girlish and so amazingly irritating.

I suddenly get the strange feeling that maybe my sister is here in the room. Invisible, like me. Hunkered down by the filing cabinet. In the messy pile of empty boxes in the corner.

But, no, I can see so much. I can see everything. I can see dust, the dry skin on Mum's nose, a tiny feather stuck to my dad's hair. I'd definitely see the apparition of another person, crouched under the window, in the corner or behind the couch.

Mostly I wonder if she looks for me. Or if maybe she just feels like something is missing. Something isn't right.

I sit back, close my eyes. Rock.

Wait, Robin Hood? What are they doing? Some kind of new game?

I crawl out from under the table to look. I stand behind my dad. His screen is scrolling numbers fast. Is that what programming looks like? It makes me feel carsick, like hairpin curves in long roads taken too fast.

"Don't take too much," says Mum. "Remember last time? That was too much, someone must have noticed. We agreed to only much smaller fractions of pennies."

"I know," he says. "Relax. It can't be traced."

Traced?

Oh my God.

Oh my God.

Oh my God.

My parents are robbing a bank.

I crawl back under the table. I try to think, but it's hard to think when I'm invisible. It's hard to make sense. My parents — *my* parents — are bank robbers.

Last time?

This time?

The last time?

How many banks have they robbed? What are they doing with the money? Not buying me new cars, that's for sure. Who are they giving it to?

I stand up again, and watch. The money looks like it's going out of one account into another. I can't see where it's going. Maybe they aren't keeping it.

"Think of it as charity," Dad says. "Take from the rich, give to the poor."

"Is it really like that?" says Mum. "Or is it just that we're selfish and want our daughter to be well taken care of?"

"It's both," says Dad firmly. "The big banks don't need this money. They won't notice it's gone. And it will make her life better. Everyone's life better who is in that place. It's the right thing to do."

That place?

I'm reeling. Bank robbers. I half-expect sirens to suddenly sound, the room to be bathed in red and blue light, teams of SWAT members to crawl through the windows.

I sit back down again.

I stay there for some time: an hour? More? Until I start to feel so weak that I think I might sleep, and who knows if I would suddenly reappear while I'm sleeping? Have to explain why I was there, crouched under the table?

I go upstairs. And I let myself come back, but only in the privacy of my room. It's funny, my room is starting to feel smaller and smaller to me. Almost like I've already grown up and left home, and am only now coming back to visit and remembering who I was. Someone I'm not anymore. So when I catch sight of my reflection in the mirror, it surprises me that I still look like me. I still look younger than I am. My hair, my skin, everything is the same.

How can I look the same?

I'm not.

TONY

11

MUM WENT BACK to work. I can't believe it. This morning when I got back from rowing practice, dripping with sweat from the run home from the docks, she startled me in the kitchen. She was wearing an actual suit. Dark grey. Pressed. No evidence of dog hair. Stockings with no runs. A shirt underneath her jacket that looked hopeful: a colourful silky one that I hadn't seen her wear for longer than I can remember. She had on makeup. I could tell because there was a chunk of black mascara clinging to her bangs. I reached over and picked it off for her. She smiled.

Smiled.

Her heels click-clacked on the floor. She ate breakfast like nothing was unusual, kissed me on the sweat-soaked cheek, which she hasn't done for months. Like she did it every day. Like she hadn't been lying on the couch for-ever. Crying.

Before I knew it, before I could figure out exactly what to say, she was gone, walking down the drive to her car.

Holding her leather briefcase. Swinging it.

I felt almost disoriented, like I was still dreaming or imagining it. But no, it was real. The car started and pulled away. There was a lump in my throat like I was going to cry, but I didn't let myself. I've been crying too easily lately. Too much.

I have to suck it up. Get over it. Move on. Focus on the future. Give myself the kind of pep talk that Coach gives us before a regatta. I got into the shower fast, like hurrying through the routine of it would make me stop thinking so much. Would make the strange feeling stop as suddenly as it began.

In the past few days, something has been in the air. Not just the actual air, although it is heavy outside, like a thunderstorm is coming. Darker than it should be. But it's more than that. I can't pinpoint it. I just feel like something's wrong. My spidey senses tingling.

Last night, I saw Israel and Michael, heads together: his dark, hers so blonde. They looked like models in a commercial for Abercrombie or something. They were talking so close, his lips must have been on her ear. Touching her skin.

Israel's been avoiding me, really obviously. I'm not imagining it; I couldn't be. Maybe I deserve it. I was a dick to him the other day and obviously he was reeling about all the stuff with his parents and I wasn't there for him. I owed him more than that. After all, he was there for me. He's like my fucking brother and I was a jerk.

I waited for him like always after school to give him a ride, but then I saw him climbing into Michael's Jeep. Casually tossing his bag into the back like he did it every day. Didn't even glance in my direction, and I felt like an asshole, sitting there in the car with my engine idling, waiting for nothing.

Stupid, but I felt jealous. Not of him, but of her. Fuck it. He's *my* friend, isn't he? Don't friends come first? Blood brothers? We did that, you know, when we were drinking one time. We were getting sappy about our friendship in a way that would never have happened if we were sober. Little kid stuff that is taboo when you're not, well, a little kid. That thing where you cut your thumb with a pocket knife and hold it against your friend's thumb and swear that forever, no matter what, you'll be friends.

Even when I'm pissed off at him, I still kind of need that.

But I still think I had a right to be mad.

And I am mad. I feel mad at everyone, as if my anger is bubbling under my skin like some kind of acne about to erupt everywhere. People are acting strangely. Wrong. Like everyone is playing out of position. Rowing port when they usually row starboard. Playing defence when they are normally on the offensive line. Making it so I don't know how to act, to react.

For example, Samantha was texting me yesterday, stuff that she shouldn't have been saying. Stuff that sounded wrong coming from her to me, or to anyone for that matter. Like she saw it in a movie and she thought it would make her seem hot, when it just made her seem awkward. Messages like, **me + you = hot**. I couldn't even look her in the eye. Hyperaggressive girls like that freak me out. It's like being hunted.

What gives with that? I don't think we've ever even really talked before, except in passing. Except that she's always been around the same people as me.

I get that we're all older and all that. More mature. Whatever. Can't we just get through this year, this last year of school, and then all go our separate ways and not have to care about one another anymore?

I've gotta admit, it's more than bugging me that Michael and Is are ... well, what are they? I don't know. It's not like she's "mine" or something. I didn't even call her. What kind of person am I, anyway? A jerk, that's who.

I just didn't know how to do it. I mean, I knew *how* to do it but I didn't know how to follow through. I couldn't do it. I couldn't picture us together, there just wasn't anything there. There wasn't enough. She's pretty, she thinks I'm cute or whatever, but still, it didn't click.

How can you call someone up and say that? I was just waiting for the right time, and it didn't come.

And now she's with Israel, so I guess I'm off the hook.

It scares me a bit that I don't feel more toward Michael. Like maybe I'm more like Joe than I thought — more removed, distant, disconnected. But then I look at my parents. Did they ever "like" each other? Did my mum ever jump on the phone when Dad called? Did Dad feel anything when he kissed her that was something different than just biology?

It all makes me feel disoriented. Mad. At myself, mostly.

And maybe I do like someone.

Maybe I like Yale. I remember that one day, when I saw her running. I liked her then, even though "liked" isn't a strong enough word. I just fell for her. And to be honest, it didn't go away. She looked so ... I don't know. I was attracted to her. I am attracted to her. She has those eyes, those amazing eyes. And besides, there's something about her.

Even though I know it's all wrong. And it would be social suicide, too. I know that. I'm not an idiot. Great way to end my school year, trying to hook up with the girl that everyone hates for being too human, for messing up. Lately she's just looked so sad. I guess I could have a thing for sad girls.

And Michael? For a second there, I thought she was sad, and then I realized she was just shallow. She sure took up with Is pretty quickly and he's my best friend. That's bad, no matter how you look at it. Bad of both of them. Really rude, to say the least.

I guess maybe I'm a bad kisser. Maybe that was all it took. It's not like I have so much practice, but I've been around. I mean, it wasn't my first kiss and no one has complained before.

I just ...

I *understand* sports. Sports are easy. You get into the boat, you row. You go to the basketball court, you shoot some hoops. Simple.

I don't know what else to do but I have to do *something* so I go into my room and throw on some clothes. Then I dig the letters from the colleges out again and look at them closely. Maybe that is the answer, after all. There's nothing for me *here*, anyway. Maybe if I go somewhere and row and win, then I'll be someone other than Israel's best friend. I'll be *me*. Myself.

I guess I'd be dumb not to get one thing for sure: Michael's eye probably was always on Israel. He's The One. The one all the girls want. He's the big star.

I hate that I feel jealous about it. I hate that it pisses me off. Hate it so much that I want to punch something. I want something to hurt more than just my muscles from working out. Like really hurt. Bones crunching. Bleeding.

I don't. But I do.

Man, I'm so messed up.

The things I don't understand could fill a book. Like my mum. My dad. Joe. Michael. Israel. Samantha.

Yale.

The sad, fucked-up thing is that I'm mad at everyone for just not getting me at all. Not that there is much to get, but somehow it feels like no one in the whole world knows me. Like the "real" me, whoever that is.

Who am *I*? I have no one to ask.

I miss my brother. He was a fuck-up, sure. But he never would have stabbed me in the back.

Although I guess he did, didn't he? In the end, he did it worse than anyone.

I grab my keys and head out, drive back down to the rowing club. I should be at school but I can't bring myself to go. And I need to work out. I need to do it in a way that I can't fight. In a way, it's like an addiction. The exhaustion point. The pushing. I'll get on the erg — the rowing machine. I can work out so hard that the ringing in my ears will stop. I'll go ten kilometres. That's a long way. That'll take a long time. And at the end of it, I'll be exhausted. I'll be able to sleep the rest of the day away. I'll be so tired that none of this will matter.

Not as much, anyway.

Michael

12

Michael doesn't know why she thought that going on this ski trip would be a good idea. She'd had an idea, way back then (has it only been a couple of weeks?) when she signed up that she and Tony would be together. She imagined digital pictures that she'd frame and hang on her wall later. A shot of them in the snow, laughing, her hair in two braids sticking out from under her new pale blue cashmere toque. Something she would take with her to college, to remember her high school boyfriend, to intimidate the boyfriends still to come with his good looks. His height. His athleticism.

Well, that's over. That whole idea has evaporated into thin air. Pictures *are* being taken, but she doesn't want anything to do with them. Not with Israel's face pressed against hers. Not with her expression of frigid barely concealed dislike that she's sure she can't hide. Besides, she has a blemish on her chin that is as glaring as a signal on a lighthouse. Disgusting.

She ruined it. Everything. Her skin (probably that chocolate sundae she ate last week, which is probably also the reason for her tightening pants, her overall bulgy awfulness). Tony. Her *plan*. Tony won't be The One now. Her idea backfired horribly, his interest in her did not pick up at the sight of her with Israel. He still hasn't called. Never called. Probably never intended to call. And now she's stuck with Israel (better than being alone, probably; at least socially it is) but she's not going to let *him* be The One. No way. For one thing, he'd make fun of her for being a virgin. Or worse, he wouldn't believe her.

Israel's hands are all over her now, the bus jostling them closer and closer together. She can practically feel the sweat through her two hundred dollar jeans. They're so soft, but he's wrecking even her satisfaction with the luxurious feeling of her clothing, his hands rubbing and rubbing them like he's trying to rub a faded pattern into the front. She moves her legs anxiously and then grabs hold of one of his hands, firmly puts it on his own thigh.

"What?" he says.

"Just don't," she says. "Just don't."

"Huh?" He looks completely confused.

"Don't touch me like that," she says. "Just don't."

Girls she doesn't even know are looking at her enviously. Do they really envy this? If they knew how uncomfortable she was, they sure wouldn't want to trade spots. They probably think they know what she's thinking; probably imagine it all wrong, much like she imagined all the scenes with Tony completely incorrectly. They don't understand that she needs *space* and she can't breathe and he keeps doing it and doing it and she's stuck. Trapped. He's not even talking to her; he's talking to everyone else. Like she's not even there. She feels both invisible and too visible. He's so loud. So obnoxious. She steals a sidelong look at Sam, across the aisle, but Sam is ignoring her completely. Pretending to read a magazine. Still hasn't forgiven her for all the stuff about Yale, how Michael defended the girl. She squints. Her head hurts. She can't remember now why that was important. She can't think. The bus is shaking from side to side. Rattling. Like it's going to fall apart at the next corner, going over the next bump. Just disintegrate, throwing them all up into the air, tossing them down onto the highway.

She chews her gum hard, swapping out for a fresh piece every few minutes; the sharp sting of the cinnamon makes her feel like she's in control. Somehow. Even though she's not. At least her breath is fresh. Sizzling. Biting.

Israel's hand refuses to stay still and everywhere he is touching her feels uniquely offended. Her skin is creeping and crawling and positively slithering away from his fingers.

"Cute sweater," she says to Aurelia, in front of her. "Totally fetch." Lately, she's been trying to reintroduce old language and she heard "fetch" in a movie on late-night TV. "Wicked," she adds.

"I totally think so, too," says Madison, half-turning around. "Fetch."

It kind of repulses Michael that as soon as she says something, Madison repeats it. She wants to yell, "Get a life!" but at the same time, it's flattering.

She wishes she didn't feel so mixed up.

To shut it off, she jams her iPod earphones in. The hands are relentless, but when she can't hear anything, she feels better. It's just her in a cloud of cinnamon gum and the music, breathing. Her heart beating to the beat of the song makes it seem like it's less work to just keep going. Keep functioning. She closes her eyes.

She knows Tony — even with the bad kiss, she still wishes things were different — is looking at her in disgust. Of course, he's disgusted. Israel is his best friend. He's disgusted with both of them, he must be, or he wouldn't be human. He must be so mad. Or worse, confused.

She hates that she's hurt him. Hates all of this. Wants to redo it differently. Wants to say "no" to Israel. Wants to start over.

With her eyes shut, she can see Tony in her mind's eye. How it could have been.

How it should have been.

Still, she wasn't good enough, just like she feared. Not good enough for him, anyway. He made that clear by freezing her out. Not calling. Acting like none of it happened, like the kiss never even happened. Like she doesn't exist.

She's feeling a bit like she doesn't, actually. She's losing it, whatever "it" is. She's losing her grip on The Girls, losing her interest in them, frankly. She's lost Tony. She's feeling somehow like she's slipping up in some irreversible way. Like she's losing herself.

Even through her closed eyes, the light is too bright. It's so sunny outside it's impossible to believe that there is snow anywhere, that sooner or later they will be skiing. The bus smells close and musty. Her head throbs. A car in the next lane is playing a radio so loudly that the bus vibrates; she can hear their song as loudly as the one in her ears.

At least her clothes look okay. She still looks good, even though everything inside her feels wrong. It makes her feel better to know that she's dressed okay. It makes her feel safe, like if she wears the same clothes as Hilary Duff or Cameron Diaz, she'll be safe like them. Protected by pretty. Somehow.

But from what?

Her breath catches. What the hell is she so afraid of, anyway? She's seventeen years old. All *this* is supposed to be fun.

She tries to relax. Concentrates on breathing. In and out, in and out. Meditation. Hope would be proud.

Skiing is fun, she tells herself. *Skiing is good*. She's a decent skier, has taken plenty of lessons. Can even do some sort of fancy tricks with moguls, fancy enough to be impressive but not so dope that the boys will feel stupid.

Sam texts her a note that says, nice teeth, loser with arrows pointing at who knows who. Michael reads it, looks sharply at Sam to see if Sam is forgiving her or maybe she just hit the wrong button. Sam's face is impassive. Maybe she was talking about Michael's teeth.

Aurelia calls something to Sam and Sam laughs so hard that her whole body shakes. She leans over the aisle to get closer to Aurelia, practically crouching on Michael's lap. Her breath is greasy, like old French fry oil. Her bad breath is pressing in on Michael, squeezing her temples.

Breathe, she thinks. *Breathe, breathe, breathe already*.

Israel's hand shifts to her waist and she slaps it away.

"Don't," she says loudly. Like she means it, really, this time.

Touching her in some places is gross but okay, but never, ever, ever that little bit of flesh that sits on top of the waistband of her jeans when she's sitting. Never that.

"Baby," he says. Or at least that's what she thinks he

says; her music is too loud to really hear. "Baby, baby, baby."

By the time they get there, she's dizzy from breathing too much or too little. From holding her breath or not. Her skin feels clammy; she needs a shower so badly, but then she'll have to redo her hair and makeup and the idea of that seems exhausting. They spill off the bus, all of them, looking like toddlers who are breaking free of their nursery school. Talking too loud, laughing too hard. Drawing too much attention — when did she ever think attention was too much? The resort is small, but groups of people are here and there. Watching the colourful, noisy boisterousness of them. Rolling their eyes, probably. Not staring in admiration as she'd once have thought. She used to believe that, anyway.

What has changed?

She puts her head down. The snow crunches under her boots. Her breath hangs in front of her mouth like a reminder that she's still doing it, still breathing. Spicy cinnamon fresh.

"I can't *wait* to find our rooms," Israel whispers in her ear. Which makes her jump and shudder, not at all with longing. More with disgust. How did he come to be so close all the time? One hook-up and that's it, her fate is sealed? And why does *he* get to choose?

She shoots him her most withering look, but it bounces off him like a basketball off a backboard. He flashes his brilliant smile, eyes crinkling at the corners. She melts a bit. Who wouldn't? No one should be as cute as him. It isn't normal. No one should be that easygoing. That impermeable. No one should be able to duck out of the way of her glare.

But he does.

"Yeah," she says, reluctantly being dragged along. "Can't wait."

A car crunches past them, spraying up slush. The trouble, of course, with spring skiing is that the snow is melting faster and faster, the roads all thick with brown sludgy slush. Not pretty. Not picture perfect.

She hitches her arms firmly through Aurelia's on one side, Madison's on the other. Forces her white sparkling smile to her lips. "C'mon, girls!"

"You are so lucky," hisses Aurelia. "First Tony and now Israel. It's not fair."

Michael shrugs. "They aren't so great," she says. She wants to say more but she doesn't.

"Sure, you can say that," says Madison enviously. "You *would* say that. You're such a bitch." But she says it affectionately. Longingly.

"Takes one to know one," says Michael.

The Girls' room is at the top of the chalet. Of course. Four beds for the four girls, like it was made up especially for them, dorm style. A bottle of water and a bowl of fruit on each nightstand. Who eats that much fruit? They don't even have to ask for it, it seems like they always get special treatment. Like they're celebrities, only they aren't. Normally Michael takes this for granted, but just now it makes her feel off-balance.

She lies down. The bed is hard and uncomfortable. She closes her eyes, the other girls racing around, unpacking, ironing or curling their hair. The smell of hot hair appliances saturating the potpourri of the air. Her hair is getting rumpled on the pillow, but for once she can't bring herself to care. She almost *wants* to look ugly.

She can't keep her eyes closed. Can't shake the idea that someone is watching her. A creepy feeling. Ghost fingers crawling on her skin.

"It's creepy here," she says.

"It's super nice, I think," says Aurelia. "I came here with Mummy and Daddy before Christmas. Wait until you see the hot tubs. Wicked. Let's go eat."

"Eat!" says Sam. "I can't eat. I'm too fat." She pinches her nonexistent belly. "Gross."

"You aren't fat," says Michael automatically.

"Let's call the boys and see what they're doing," says Aurelia. "I'm so over this part already. The bus? Deadly. *So* over it."

"I'm tired," says Michael. "I think I have a headache."

"No, you don't," says Aurelia. "You just need to get changed, fix your makeup. Come on! It will be great." Her tone broaches no room for argument.

Michael drags herself up, feeling like she's moving through mud. Maybe she's getting sick. But not like the flu. Something really bad. Like leukemia or herpes or something. Something gross. Something that gets into your blood and kills you, or at least ruins your life. Something that makes you ugly. In the bathroom, she splashes cold water on her face. She's seen this in movies, on commercials. It always looks pretty, refreshing. Frankly, it never results in what she sees in front of her: smeared mascara, skin showing under her makeup. Bags under her unconcealed eyes. Hair flattened at the top. She sighs and reapplies. Fixes her hair. Takes her time, The Girls can wait. They're used to waiting for her. She is, after all, in spite of Sam's defection, the leader. She's still the prettiest. No matter what.

She can hear them shrieking in the other room. It sounds like a pillow-fight. Sometimes she wishes … well, she wishes they weren't so immature. She wishes they'd leave her alone. She'd take a bath. Watch some TV. Go to bed.

Alone.

She can hear boys' voices now intermingled with the girls. Great, she thinks. They're here.

She brushes her teeth, fixes her lip gloss. Looks at herself in the mirror. At least she looks the part, she thinks. At least she has it half-right. Forces herself to smile, shoulders back, spine ramrod straight like the ballerina she was as a child. She launches herself back into the fray.

By dark, they are all drunk. Outside. It's snowing. Cold, but she doesn't really feel it. Oh, that's because she's in the hot tub. She only barely remembers getting in. The burning of the water on her skin.

The taste of wine is bitter in her mouth. In the reflection in the window, her teeth look black.

Where are the teachers? The chaperones? Michael squints into the shadows. She can't see any of them but they must be around. Submerged in the hot tub, she's boiling hot. Sweating. She must look like a lobster. Awful.

Israel has gone somewhere. Where? She can't remember. Oh, to take a *piss*. That's right. That's what he said.

Gross.

Although it's a good thing because when he isn't pressing in on her, she can breathe better. She should probably get out of this tub before she gets too hot, passes out, drowns. But she's too drunk. Leans her head back and rests it on a towel. The night is dark and starry. Pretty. Cold. Crisp. Yet so clear. Where is everyone else? She frowns. Her posse has left her side, she can hear them yelling and screaming. The stars pepper the sky like an infinite number of holes filled with light.

Oh, that's right. Tobogganing. The Girls went tobogganing. The whole act of doing that seemed cold and messy. She bowed out and they all left, everyone. Giving her and Is time alone. He was demanding it. He was telling them to go. It felt wrong, but she didn't stop them. She felt so foggy.

Alone with Israel.

Oh, that's worse than tobogganing, she thinks. But it's too late to toboggan and the heat of the tub is making her feel so sleepy.

Then, with a splash, he is back in the water, head under the surface, bursting back through like a whale breaching.

"You're so hot," he says, lurching toward her face. Is that supposed to be sweet? She shakes her head, and he assumes that she means she isn't.

"What do you mean?" he says. "You're the hottest of all the girls here. Everyone wants you."

"I know," she says, which comes out bitchier than anything, but who cares. She doesn't care what he thinks of her.

"Tony thinks you're hot," he says.

"I wish," she says.

"What?" he says.

"Nothing," she says.

"I get it," he says. "You're just with me to get to him."

"No," she says honestly. "He just wasn't into me."

"Bullshit," says Israel. "That's bullshit." Then he moves in for the kiss. She's too drunk for this, she thinks. His hands, tongue, everything are everywhere like a sea creature with too many suction pads, wet and sloppy and all over, impossible to remove.

"Stop," she says.

"Come on, baby," he says. Where does he get his lines? They're so dumb. They're so trite. She slaps at him, and he pushes her arm away like a twig.

Suddenly her vision tunnels. She feels like she's watching herself from far, far, far away, too far away to help herself.

"Stop it," she says. "I have to get out. It's too hot in here."

"You're too hot," says Israel. His tongue is attacking her. Horrible. She pushes at him.

"Get off," she says. She's getting scared. Her voice sounds like it's being held under a mute button. Muffled. "Stop it."

He is up in one motion, pulling her out of the tub. Then what? She's not sure how it's happening, they are beside the tub and he is on her.

It's hurting.

He is hurting her.

She's pushing at him. She must be at least scratching him but his body is like a stone statue, impermeable. She can't move him.

She can't breathe.

She's gasping for air.

"Fuck off," she says. "Get off me."

She can't move.

She's definitely crying. God, it hurts.

Bile is rushing into her mouth. *Good*, she thinks, *if I throw up he'll stop*. She dry heaves, but he doesn't stop. He keeps going. She starts to black out.

Her body a million miles away, like she's been transported up to one of those stars and can only just barely see herself in the distance.

His hands are pulling her, pushing her. Bruising her skin. Why is she naked? She's so cold, or is she?

Someone else is shouting. And then he's off her. She rolls away. Closes her eyes. Shivering, she can't move.

Oh, no. This isn't right.

There are *people*. There are people, more and more of them, gathering, shouting. *Watching*. She closes her eyes tight, wills herself not to cry or vomit or somehow embarrass herself even more. She has no idea what to do now. No idea. She can feel snow under her hands. Where did it come from? She's freezing. Is she dying?

Who are the *people*? Her friends? If so, why aren't they propping her up, wrapping her in something warm, getting her out of there?

Why isn't anyone helping her?

"She's passed out," someone says. And she wills herself to do it, wills herself to let go so she's gone, everything black, and she's so relieved and is she really passed out? Yes, she is. Nothing now. Nothing left.

Not now.

Not tonight.

Someone is lifting her, dragging her. That's okay, then. Someone's got her, after all.

Yale

13

When I realized what my parents were doing, I confronted them. Not like I wanted to, because I chickened out and, besides, they weren't really reacting the way I thought they would. You know when you storm into a room and you're planning to say something, something really meaningful, and then you expect the person you are addressing to say a certain thing and they don't say it? And you're kind of left hanging? It was like that.

I guess I started with, "I know you're robbing banks." I felt like I was in a bad movie, to be honest. I felt like I was reading a line.

Mum was sipping coffee at the table, flipping through the classifieds. Dad was frying an egg. His hair was sticking up all over like he'd done it on purpose with mousse, but from the imprint of a keyboard on his cheek I could tell it was more that he'd just fallen asleep at his desk. Again.

They didn't really answer. Or react. I kind of thought they'd yell or get mad or deny it or something. Anything.

"It's not really robbing," said Mum. "It's more a transfer of funds."

"Yeah," said Dad. "Want an egg?"

"What?" I said. "What?"

"Want an egg?" he repeated.

"No!" I said quietly. "I do not want an egg. Are you fucking crazy?" They both looked up at me. I almost never swear, not in front of them. "You can't just rob banks. I'm sorry, but you can't."

"Well, we *did*," said Mum. "We don't have to ask your permission. It's for a good cause."

"I don't care!" I said. "This is ridiculous. Who do you think you are?"

"Calm down," said Dad.

"I am calm," I said, as calmly as I could.

"You don't sound calm," said Mum.

"Are you from a different planet?" I yelled. "Are you insane?"

"No," said Mum. "And no."

"This is crazy!" I was really freaking out. I mean, who wouldn't? It was beyond ridiculous. Not just the robbing, but the nonreaction. Like everyone is idly robbing banks in their spare time? I don't think so.

"You could go to jail," I said. "Did you ever think what would happen to me?"

"We won't get caught," said Dad. "It isn't possible. Besides, we've stopped."

"Oh," I said. "I guess that makes it A-okay, then."

"Not really," said Mum. She was starting to look worried, to give her credit. Although she was probably mostly worrying about the burning egg. "It's just that we have to do it. For Yale."

"For Yale," I repeated.

"For Yale," Dad said.

"For Yale," said Mum.

"Yeah," I answered. "So you said."

So she explained that Yale was … well, pretty disabled. Really disabled. Severely disabled. So disabled that she needs twenty-four hour care, tubes, oxygen. Beyond disabled. Just, really, barely alive.

As she was talking, I could feel the room starting to swim. The table shifting. Nothing holding still. I guess I fainted. And then, when I came to, I stayed lying still for a while. Eyes closed. I could hear them talking still, speculating about whether they should wake me up or call 911. I opened my eyes and sat up. I felt so incredibly, overwhelmingly sad, I can't even explain it. It's stupid, I guess. I somehow had decided that "not well" meant she was like Sully. Well enough, but not present. I hadn't imagined that "not well" meant "completely dependent on tubes and tanks." I hadn't pictured "severely disabled." It was like I couldn't process the information. Every time I tried to think about it directly, a pain started in my chest that felt like a pencil being thrust through my heart.

"The money keeps the hospital where she lives open," said Mum. "We had to do it." Then she turned the last page of the paper, folded it up and chucked it in the recycling.

"Horrible," I muttered. And I made myself get up, even though my head felt like a balloon floating somewhere up near the ceiling. "Horrible."

I felt so mad. But I can't even pinpoint why. It had something to do with my dad taking a big bite of the fried egg sandwich, yolk dripping down his chin. My mum's well-that's-that-then look that wrapped it all up and dismissed it. The tiny kitchen that stunk like air freshener and bad milk. It was too much.

I stumbled out the front door, threw up in a pot of half-dead tulips and just started to run. I had to run, see, because it stopped me from thinking about anything else.

I ended up here, on the bus to the ski hill. With all these kids from school who I don't want to see. I don't want to be here.

But I don't want to be anywhere, so here (or not here) is as good a place as any. I mean, I'm disappeared. As far as they know, I'm not here. As far as my parents know, I'm not there.

So I'm not anywhere. I'm nowhere. Just like my sister, I guess. But in a different way.

I can't believe they can't see me. I have to sit on the floor at the end of the aisle. I feel so visible, but no one looks. I have a strange feeling like I could reappear and yet still be invisible. Like I've become so much in the background that people would forget to see me, somehow. But that isn't true, not for real. I am always too visible. Everyone is always too ready with a tampon joke. I am The Bleeder. Let's not forget *that*. Not for a second. Never.

The mood on the bus is too tight, mirroring something I'm feeling inside but can't quite identify. You can practically see it, the laughter all strung out like strings of coloured lights about to snap, broken glass about to fly everywhere. It makes me nervous, or maybe I'm just sick with nervousness already. "Nervousness" isn't even the right word for it. I don't know what the right word is.

Everyone is too loud, fake happy; too look-at-us-aren't-we-good-friends. Too many cameras snapping pictures. It feels constricting, like the air is cotton candy. It smells like overheated bodies, toothpaste, laundry soap, musty ski jackets.

I wonder what anyone is getting out of this. It is like they are performing for an audience, only no one is watching. They are too busy being the-kid-having-the-most-fun-of-all.

I guess I'm wrong when I say no one is watching. I'm watching. Watching Tony watching Michael watching Israel watching watching ... Sort of like watching TV, only it's all real. They are all so creepily attractive, like wax figurines. The key players in the show. Top billing.

Honestly, it is almost sick the way the other kids, the less popular kids, take their pictures. Like The Girls are stars and they are paparazzi. Paris Hilton and Nicole Richie. It's gross is what it is. And yet I can't stop looking at them either.

For fun, I let my hand come back into view. I want someone to notice. To be scared. At least if someone is scared of me, I'll know I am still here.

No one sees.

I'd forgotten for a while how much I hate bus rides, how buses make me feel faint, dizzy, light-headed. Sick. But it doesn't take long for the feeling to come to me, for me to remember. I feel panicky. What if I faint and no one sees me? Or worse, what if I faint and come back into view, suddenly appearing where no one was before? What would they do?

I dig my nails into my palm. Will myself to not panic, to stay conscious. I count my breathing, my pulse, the seats, shoes, bags, blonde heads, brunettes. I count to distract myself and to keep myself present. It's hard to stay gone for the whole interminable ride. Two hours. My bladder is screaming pain; I have to pee so bad. I'm so hot-cold, I can't even tell which I am anymore. It's too long. I'm panicking, breathing too fast; I can't stay disappeared much longer.

When we finally arrive, I'm relieved. The bus grinding to a lurching halt. People spilling off. That's when I realize what a mess I've gotten myself into. I can't stay gone, but I can't reappear here, either. I'm not supposed to be on this trip.

Where will I sleep? I can't stay invisible while I sleep, I don't think. It would be too scary. What if I couldn't come back?

My whole body is shaking like I have hypothermia. The kids are taking forever to get off the bus. Oh, hurry, hurry. I can't do this. Not much more.

What had I been thinking?

I don't know.

I just had to do it.

Right before I left, I did this really strange thing. I grabbed a glass of milk that Mum had on the table and I threw it at her. Not the glass, just the milk. It spiralled through the air like some white, opaque bird. Splatted all over her face.

And then I ran.

I wanted to see Michael. Knowing that she had a brother, Sully, who wasn't well either. Like she could relate to me now, not that I'd ever tell her. She just felt suddenly safe to me. Like a place I needed to get to. Somewhere I needed to be.

So I got two hours to stare at her on the bus. Being pretty. Probably not thinking about her brother at all. Probably not thinking how lucky she was to be so normal. Not even normal, but perfect.

Israel Santiago attached to her side like a slug.

Tony a few seats back, across the aisle, pretending it wasn't bothering him, but it was. I could see it in the muscles in his neck, in his leg tapping too hard and too fast against the back of the seat in front of him. Not that the girl in front of him would have the nerve to turn around and tell him to stop. Matti beside him, every once in a while whooping like he was watching a sporting event and someone got a goal or a touchdown or hole-in-one, even though no TV was on.

It took half the bus trip for my pulse to slow down to something close to normal. For me to feel like I wasn't going to die. I wonder if anyone has ever died from fury. Or confusion.

I don't understand, I don't understand, I don't understand. My parents. Their secret lives. Yale. "You get what you get." How can they live with it? I don't know what I want them to do, but more. More than their stupid skateboards and Greenpeace tattoos. All those lies and that fake *caring*: she was inconvenient and they didn't want to deal.

What if there had been something wrong with me? Something more than there is, I mean. Something more than what they don't know.

Finally the bus is empty. I just need a bathroom. A place to reappear. Soon. I follow The Girls. Then, at the last minute, decide the boys are a better bet. Less observant. Easier to hide from. And I'm curious, I admit it.

Curious to see what they talk about when they think they're alone. Curious what Tony's like when he's with his buddies. Curious, curious.

Curiosity killed the cat, I guess. I should have kept that in mind.

The boys' room is like a different world: just a bunch of furniture, but they fill it up extra. Somehow extra noisy, extra smelly, extra everything. Sharing this room are Israel, Tony, Matti and Jackson Phillips. I reappear — finally, finally, like surfacing after an impossibly deep dive — in their closet, guessing (rightly) that they won't be hanging anything up. Their conversation is actually pretty mundane, talking about skiing, which run is the best, skimming the surface. It takes me a while to register that Israel is talking about Michael, after all. The way he's talking, well, I had thought he was talking about some kind of sport. Something he could win.

"I'm gonna score," he says. "Big time. This is it, boys and girls. This is the big show."

"You go, big guy," says Matti.

"Lucky bastard," says Jackson. "She's so hot."

At first Tony ignores them, and then he says sharply, "What?"

"I'm going for it," says Israel. "Wish me luck, brother."

"Does Michael know?" says Tony. "Is she in on your plan? Because I don't think she's that into you. You heard her on the bus. She didn't even want your hands on her."

"You don't know what you're talking about," says Israel. "She knows she wants me."

He goes to the mirror and makes a gesture to himself, hip thrusting, obnoxious.

"You're an asshole," says Tony.

"What's it to you?" says Israel. "You're the one who never even called her."

Tony looks like he's about to smash Israel in the face. I've never seen him look like that.

They take longer to get ready to go somewhere than girls do. They take forever in the bathroom. The stench of it nearly makes me gag.

While he waits, Matti lies on a bed and idly plays with himself through his pants like no one will notice. Israel pops a zit with huge concentration. I can see it all through the door, which is ajar. It is both boring and disgusting. And these people make fun of me for getting my period? I don't get how that works. Tony is lying on his bed; I can see his jaw grinding. He's not talking but I can tell he's stewing. He's really mad. I want to know what he's thinking. Is it that he's jealous or is he really afraid for Michael?

Somehow, *I'm* afraid. For her. Israel is just so *feral*.

I'm getting jumpy with nerves. I need a cigarette. It's weird because clove cigarettes don't have the nicotine that other cigarettes do. They aren't supposed to be addictive. But I am addicted to their smell. To the feeling of drawing in the hot, spicy burn of them. But I can't do that when I am disappeared. Can't do anything. And I can't reappear here at the mountain. How could I explain my arrival?

I spend a lot of time waiting for the boys to get it together and to get out. I know they will, I just wish they'd hurry up. I need the room to myself for a while.

To be visible.

To smoke.

To eat.

To *pee*.

They are finally gone, a tumble out the door, fake wrestling (mostly Matti just jumping on everyone's back), real tension (Israel and Tony snarling at each other like puppies who have been playing and then suddenly realize that they wanted to draw blood). All that stuff that boys do when they think someone's looking and apparently even when someone isn't. I am so relieved to reappear that I actually cry. There's just too much going on, I can't help it. I cry and cry. And pee. Right away.

When all that's done, I dig around in their stuff. I need to eat something desperately. Tony's bag is mostly just full of clothes that all smell like fabric softener and him. I bury my nose in them and inhale. Israel's bag is similar but the smell isn't good. It isn't … I can't explain it. His stuff smells like something dark, like the water near a fuel dock: like gasoline, salt and pollution.

I finally find some power bars in Matti's stuff. A bag of Doritos. I am so hungry, my hands are shaking too hard to open the Doritos. I drink a bunch of water. Try to calm down, to get my mind back to normal so I can figure out a way to get out of this.

I can't.

I'm panicking.

I feel like I need to hurry, to get to Michael, to do something. But what? Tell her that Israel is … well, what would I say? Why would she listen, anyway? I'm sure she knows he's going to try something. She's a big girl. She can figure it out.

I just can't shake the feeling that there's something really *off* about the whole thing.

My head is wrapped in gauze. I feel like I'm going to faint.

What am I going to do?

I don't know. I don't know. I don't know.

I lie on Tony's bed. I wrap his sheets around me. This seems safe somehow. This seems like a cocoon. Then, just as quickly, too hot. Too confined.

Suddenly, I have to get outside. Into the fresh air. The cold will snap me out of this, bring me back to myself. I don't care who sees me. Does anyone care enough about me to know if I'm supposed to be on the trip or not? I doubt it. It's more important, visible or not, that I get to Michael. That I find her. Then I'll figure it out.

I follow the sounds of the voices, The Girls' voices, unmistakable. As I get close, I lose my nerve and make myself disappear again, even though it's hard. Even though I can hardly do it. It's such an effort. I feel like I want to lie down in the snow, rest my hot cheek on the cold crystals of ice.

The Girls are tumbling over one another. Shrieking and laughing. Their drunkenness is like a cloud hanging over them that they can't see. Madison throws up neatly into a bank of snow, laughing the whole time. She even makes throwing up look not gross. How is that possible?

Michael's not with them.

They vanish in the direction of the toboggan run. Shouting and laughing. Running. Like they aren't so drunk they can barely stand.

I shudder. Keep moving. Trudging along in the direction they had come from. Then I find the hot tub.

I find Michael.

She's slumped in the water, alone. I'm torn. Should I reappear?

No, I should leave her alone. She doesn't need me.

Still, I feel like I want to keep an eye on Michael, make sure she doesn't slip under the water and drown or something. Down below the patio where she is in the hot tub, in the distance I can see Tony chucking snowballs at Matti and Jackson. I go closer, to see him better. He looks relaxed and this makes me feel happy. He looks young. He doesn't always. Sometimes he looks like the oldest person I've ever seen. I guess I'm distracted by them because I don't notice Israel until he jumps into the hot tub, practically landing on Michael's head.

Then he starts to …

I have to …

What do I do now?

Then she starts to fight him, and he's pulling her out of the water. For a minute, I'm paralyzed. I can't move. I'm too far away to get to her quickly, how did I move so far away? Drawn to Tony like a magnet.

She's saying something. She's saying "no." Can no one else hear this?

Then I hear a scream. It's so loud. Like something tearing the very fabric of the air, splitting it apart. It's so powerful it stops me from moving, and then I realize that it's me. Is it me?

I've reappeared. I don't even know what I'm doing, but my foot makes solid contact with Israel's back. Michael doesn't seem to see me at all. She's clawing at him and I'm hurting him, or at least it's hurting my fists to strike him. My nails break on his skin.

There are people coming toward us but all I can think about is keeping Israel off Michael, which is harder than you might think. He's so strong, he keeps flinging me aside, but he can't really be meaning to go back to what he was doing. She's lying there, shivering, shivering, blue around the lips like she's dying. Time feels all wrong. Things are moving too slowly. His fist lands solidly on my jaw, which hurts more than I'd ever imagined a punch would hurt. I keep seeing stars, not just a few stars drifting but like I'm being hit in the face with a shower of light so bright I can't see anything.

Tony is suddenly there. There is a blast of voices so loud I can't make them out, the noise is so much that I fall back through space, a terrible distance and I think I disappear accidentally. When I figure out how to reappear, I see Tony. He's punching Israel again and again, blood everywhere, Matti on him screaming, "Don't kill him, don't kill him," and Michael lying there, eyes closed but I can see them moving. I can see she's pretending. I go over to her. I lift her up. She isn't heavy. She's like a bird, weightless, empty boned. I don't know, she feels like air.

She's floating in my grip.

Maybe I am a superhero after all.

But then I see the most shocking thing I think I've ever seen ... her friends, her so-called friends, are laughing. Aurelia hiccups loudly, changing the mood into something else. Madison waves. Sam is laughing like something is hysterically funny, holding her gut. They're drunk, but so what?

I somehow get Michael back to her room. Their room. But I lock the door and bolt it. The other girls can sleep outside, that's what they deserve. I put her in bed. I think she's awake, but she's not letting on. Her eyes are tight shut like a toddler trying to block out something on TV that she doesn't want to see. I don't know what else to do, so I crawl into one of the other beds. It takes a long time, both of us breathing, the sound of that filling up the room. I think she's crying, but I don't talk. I want her to have her privacy. I don't want to freak her out. Finally, I fall asleep myself, listening to the sound of her sobbing.

In the morning, I wake up. Confused. Don't know where I am. The sheets smell unfamiliar and are tangled around my legs like a net.

It takes me a minute, and then I remember.

Michael is awake. She's sitting on the edge of her bed, back to me. She's crying. Still or again, I don't know which.

"Don't tell anyone, Yale," she says. "Don't tell."

"Of course," I say. My mouth is so dry. Doesn't she wonder why I'm here?

"If no one knows, then it didn't happen," she says.

"Right," I say reassuringly. I don't know how to tell her that she's wrong. That everyone knows. Everyone. She must know, though; she must already know.

We sit together all the way home. For the first time ever, I don't feel faint on the bus. The bus itself doesn't make me feel sick. Not the smell, the air, nothing.

No one asks me why I'm here. Not even the teachers who look hung over themselves. Do they know?

Don't they have to count heads? I hope we didn't leave someone behind, someone whose place I'm taking. No one cares. You could cut the tension with a knife. Tony is sitting by himself at the back, sprawled over two seats. Everything about his demeanour suggests that, if you come near him, then he'll growl and spit. Israel stares out the window through one black eye. Did I do that? Somehow he still looks fierce. Impenetrable.

Innocent.

How can he not look guilty?

Sam, Aurelia and Madison whisper and stare. Whispering and staring is what they do, though this time it's subdued for them. Others are listening to music. Reading. Everyone looks dazed, like they've just survived something terrible and don't know how to process it, how to describe it, even to themselves. All over the bus, you can imagine them rewriting the story in their heads to make it okay. To make Israel — the school hero — not the bad guy.

I'm getting the feeling that it's not going to come out so well for Michael. Everyone is quick to hate and blame the pretty girl. Girls will turn on her fast, faster than you can imagine. And boys will be happy to follow along.

I glance over at Michael. Her iPod on, of course. She ignores me. Her skin is blotchy, red. Her hair is stringy. She looks like someone else. Like she's metamorphosed backward into something worse than she was, a butterfly becoming a caterpillar.

Her eyes sag at the corners, like she's lost the ability to keep them fully open.

It's a good thing she has the headphones on.

She won't hear the sound of the tide turning, the blame falling squarely on her. The story changing under her feet, leaving her with nothing solid to find her footing on. Leaving her alone.

Just like me.

TONY

14

DAD'S TAKING ME for dinner. Like this is supposed to thrill me. This is supposed to make up for the fact that he's an asshole. Just fucking delightful, I'm sure. In light of everything else, I find it hard to take it seriously. It feels like a part in a play that I'm not sure I'm even in anymore.

I wonder where he's going to take me. Chuck E. Cheese? I'm getting tired of him. I'll admit that at first I wanted him to come home, to be normal, to make everything okay. Now it's different. Mum is okay, after all, without him. He's a storm that has passed, only he doesn't realize it. He thinks we're still there waiting for his next move.

Like we care.

It's almost comical.

Now he's taking on the role of divorced dad like he's been watching too many movies: he wants to go to hockey games. Concerts. Movies. He calls my cell phone and leaves rambling messages that I can't bring myself to respond to.

Dinner is a new thing, though. I don't think we've ever done that. I feel like I have to go because he delivered the invitation in person. Showed up at the dock this morning, his awkward bulk looming out of the darkness, startling me, as the team went about the morning stuff we always do: bringing the boats down from the boathouse, hosing off the dock, chasing away the fat seals who like to sleep on it. I was so caught up in the routine that seeing him suddenly standing in front of me was like a nightmare. Out of context, it took me a minute to think of how he could be there and what he could want.

"Been having trouble reaching you," he said. He was wearing too-tight sweatpants and a Habs jersey. I hate the Habs. That's what I was thinking: *how can my father be a Habs fan?*

It didn't make sense, but nothing does. Not anything. Not anymore. Not after what happened this weekend, like a nightmare I can't get out of my head — my knuckles wrapped in tape still, probably all broken, not that I'm going to go get them X-rayed. The pain reminds me of what happened, of what I wasn't fast enough to stop. What I should have known was going to happen.

I shouldn't have let Israel out of my sight. I should have protected Michael.

I should have *known*. And I did. I did know.

My dad's presence in my space, my boathouse, my territory? That made the least sense of all.

"Phone's broken," I lied. A handful of the guys stopped what they were doing, looking at us strangely. We don't get many drop-in visitors at five in the morning, I can tell you that.

Coach hovered nearby. "All right?" he said.

"Yeah," I said. "My dad."

He shrugged, went back to attaching lights to the bows of the boats bobbing in the rippling water.

"What do you want?" I asked. "Why are you here?"

"Dinner," he said. His hands were twisting. Looked like he wanted to be holding something. He put his hands in his pockets, pulled out his keys and started tossing them in the air. "Just want to see my son for dinner tonight, is that so wrong?"

"Dad," I started. Then I heard the coach's whistle go. I didn't want to get into it. "Fine," I said over my shoulder. "Whatever."

I guess he left. I didn't look back. My heart was beating like I'd already finished the workout and I hadn't even started. Got into the boat and nearly overturned, like all my movements were too big. I felt self-conscious. But once I got going, I could make all the noises in my head shut down. Funny enough, I beat my best time trial. It was like the water was pushing me along instead of stalling my progress. Shooting me forward. So much adrenalin going through my body it felt like something was going to give, something so powerful I'd be propelled out of the boat, into the sky, into the atmosphere, gone.

I tried to forget about Dad. Put the whole thing out of my head. But now I'm waiting for him, worrying. Dinner is awkward, it means too much conversation, normally something he avoids. So the invitation itself means he's going to tell me something. Some big announcement. I fucking hate that I'm scared that he's going to say that he's getting his own place, that he's gone for good.

I want him gone. I don't know why I wouldn't.

Mum's doing so well, so much better. She can get through a whole day without crying. She's going to work.

I don't want him to fuck it up. I don't want anything to do with him. But I hate that I'm sort of looking forward to it. Like I'm a baby, a little kid. Like I should get all excited that Daddy's taking me out for a goddamn burger.

And then he doesn't show up.

"I'm sure he's coming, honey," says Mum. Standing behind me. Touching me on the arm like she wants to hug me but she doesn't remember how or maybe I'm too old now for that to be okay.

"Yeah," I say. "Sure."

I wait. I watch some TV and it's getting dark outside and he's not coming. It's always what you don't expect, you know? I thought he'd come and give me some bad news; turns out he was never coming at all.

I can't stand it. I feel like I'm going to cry or jump out of my skin. I almost want to. Want something to happen. Anything. "I'm going out," I tell Mum.

"Oh!" she says. She looks like she's going to cry, but at least she doesn't. She's getting stronger. I can see it in the iron grey of her eyes. The way her shoulders are squared, like she's going to lift or push something heavy. She looks different. Maybe it's just the lipstick. I give her a quick, awkward hug.

"Okay," she says. "Be careful."

"I'm just going for a walk," I tell her. I take my basketball though. It's comforting, you know? Head down to shoot some hoops. In the dark, in the light, what does it matter? A hundred will make me feel better. I know it. Or maybe less. Maybe just ten in a row will be enough. Maybe fifty. Maybe it doesn't matter how many. Maybe there's no formula for it, after all.

I bounce the ball as I walk. Counting without thinking. I pass Yale's house in the dark. Her scooter is parked out front. She's the hero, not me. But instead of being jealous or feeling somehow like my role was stolen, I like her more.

I have her eyes in my head and I can't stop thinking about her. I saw her carrying Michael out of there, saw it from where I was pinned under Matti. Him holding me down. Preventing me from doing what I wanted to do so bad, to Israel. What I couldn't stop myself from doing.

I guess it's good that he stopped me.

It's definitely good that Yale was there. She stopped him first.

Weird thing is, I don't remember seeing her on the bus on the way up. Don't remember her being there at all. Like in the comic books, when the heroine swoops in and saves the day. Only she wasn't naked. Didn't have huge boobs.

I lose control of the ball and it rolls across the street, I have to jog to catch up to it before it goes all the way down the hill. A dog barks viciously from behind a closed door. I jump. I'm so ratcheted up, my nerves feel like they are hopping: popcorn popping in hot oil.

I start to sprint. Counting footsteps, losing count, counting breaths, holding the ball tight like it's going to escape. Counting heartbeats. Lines in the sidewalk. Everything, anything.

Trying not to keep seeing the image of Israel's face. Israel's smirk as Yale clawed at him. Like she wasn't hurting him, only she was. She really was. He wouldn't give that away, though; not on his smug face. He tried to make it look like she didn't matter, like he was stopping because he was done. But that wasn't it.

She stopped him.

He makes me so sick, I can't stand it. My guts cramp like a balled-up fist.

Rape, right? Because that's what it was. There's no way it's anything different. There's no way she agreed to that. I think of how her hair was always so perfect. Lying there, she looked a mess. She looked so tiny, like a bird that had fallen out of its nest and couldn't fly away.

I filled out my college applications when I got home. Pretty much the minute I got in the door. I wanted to call the police, but I didn't know ... I mean, what would that start for her? It wasn't my choice to make. I also wanted to go to Israel's house and kill him. I wanted to call Michael, see if she was okay. But I didn't. Instead, I leafed through the sheaf of papers. Got out my chewed-up pen and started filling in the blanks. It was all I could think of to do. I wanted to pack a bag right then, leave this town and never look back, and that's as close as I could get. It was two in the morning and I was hunched over those application essays, writing like it was going to save someone. Like maybe it would save me.

Hank's slumped in his usual spot. For the first time ever, he lifts his hand in greeting. I wave back, stand on the foul line, start shooting. I shoot and shoot. And shoot. Over and over and over again. I don't hear Israel at first, and then he's there, next to me. On that stupid skateboard, looking cocky as ever in spite of his bruises. Coughing. Smoking a joint.

"What do you want?" I say.

"Nothing," he shrugs. "Just hanging."

"Don't hang here," I say.

"What's your bent?" he says.

"My bent," I repeat. "What's my bent?" I pass the ball to

him so hard, to the chest, it knocks the wind out of him. The joint falls into a puddle. He throws the ball back to me, a girl throw. Bounce pass. I catch it easily in one hand.

"What the fuck do you think?" I say.

"Relax," he says. "I'm not embarrassed. Why are you being such an asshole?"

"Why am I being such an asshole?" I repeat.

"Yeah," he says. "That's what I said."

"Is," I say.

"What?" he says. He's standing back a bit. Wary. Like he's going to bolt at any second. I take a step toward him.

"None of that is okay, you sick fuck," I say. "None of it is okay."

"What are you talking about?" he says. "You would have done the same. Maybe you could have. She was up for it. If it weren't for that bitch Yale, maybe we all would have got what we wanted."

"You fucking asshole," I say. I lurch toward him, tripping. Then I'm on my knees and I can tell they are bleeding. He's running. His feet hitting the pavement like hammer falls that I swear I can feel through my kneecaps. Really running.

I don't go after him. Let him figure it out for himself.

"Fuck off," I yell after him. Even though he's already gone.

In the distance, I can see him slowing to a walk. Bending over like he has a cramp. I used to think he was like liquid but now I see that he's not at all. He's just a fucked-up kid who thought he could get away with anything. And he can't. Or maybe he did.

That's what scares me the most. Maybe he just *did*.

Well, maybe he can with everyone else. But not with

me. I don't owe him that much. No way.

I don't even notice at first that I'm crying, but I am. Again. Crying like a baby. Embarrassing, chest-heaving sobs that threaten to turn me inside out.

Really crying. If anyone saw me, I'd …

Well.

Hank pats the ground next to him, and I don't know. Suddenly he looks like the friendliest face I've ever seen.

Passes me the bottle.

I drink. And I guess I keep going.

I wake up at sunrise, my face on the ground. *Ground* into the ground. Broken glass cutting into my cheek. I have no idea where I am, and then I do and I hate myself. That isn't an exaggeration. I hate myself, lying there. For the first time, ever. I think, *what will Mum think?*

This is the worst thing I've ever done. I can tell from where the sun is in the sky that I've missed rowing. I never miss rowing. Not ever. Doing it now feels like a failure.

Not that I could have rowed. My head is exploding. A blinding video game of pain so intense I think, for a second, that if I get up I'll keel right back over again. The sun is so bright, my eyes hurt so bad.

It sounds weird, but I swear that standing over me is Yale, like some kind of creepy transparent guardian angel, and then she's gone.

My mouth is like paper. So dry.

When I get home, my mum's on the couch again. She's crying. Won't talk to me. Says she was up all night worrying.

I can smell the stench of me, filling up the whole living room with reminders of Joe.

I'm such a fuck-up.

Who am I now?

Michael

15

Of course, she has to go back to school. Head held high. Like nothing happened. That's the only option. She's thought of everything. The police, but no. So what if she presses charges? It doesn't undo it. It just keeps it alive for longer and she's not up for that. She won't tell her family, they can't know. That's part of it, at least. So she can't tell.

She should have screamed louder. She should have drunk less. She should have found the strength to run. Clawed his beautiful eyes out of his head. Torn his cheeks open with her nails.

But she didn't. The cold wintery air touching her skin all over like a thousand hands. She couldn't get it off her. She couldn't get him off her. She wasn't strong enough. He won. She lost.

She hates him. With every cell in her body, she hates him. It fills her up so fully that it's hard to imagine there will ever be room inside her for anything else. She hasn't been able to eat or drink or anything and as a result of that — maybe just that, maybe that plus the trauma, the fear, the weird waves of anxiety that are rolling over her like surf — she's light-headed. Nothing feels quite real enough to matter.

"If no one knows," she whispers to herself. She wears her favourite Prada top. Kasil jeans. Frye boots. She's decked out. Her hair is perfect. But there is something wrong with her face. She knows it. It shows. Of course, it shows. It's not her skin or her makeup. It's something in her eyes. Dead fish swimming in a polluted sea.

She's ruined.

If nothing else, she knows she's going to take the fallout. It won't be Israel, she can already tell. He's too good-looking, too well-liked, too likely-to-succeed. It's going to be painted as her fault. Someone will suggest that she asked for it and people will want to believe it because she's one of The Girls.

She's a bitch.

Did she ask for it?

No, no, no. She didn't.

She told him to stop. That should have been enough, even if physically he could hold her down. Make her.

She makes her legs move. They feel like they don't belong to her. Nothing belongs to her anymore. She does not belong.

"Bye, Mike," yells her mum from the bathtub. It's so startling and loud that Michael nearly screams. She forces herself to answer.

"Bye," she says hoarsely. Her voice doesn't even sound like hers anymore.

I am still the same person, she reminds herself. *I am still breathing.*

Breathe.

Yet she can't.

What if she's pregnant? Then what? Or, worse, what if he's given her something, some disease, something awful? Something deadly?

Her knees wobble. She stands outside the bathroom door. She can smell the Body Shop bath gel her mother uses. She wants to open the door, kneel by the tub and rest her head on her mother's chest.

But that would be crazy, so she doesn't.

She makes her way down the hall. Holding on almost, hand dragging along the rough plaster wall, feeling vertigo pushing her toward the ground. Which way is up? She stops in Sully's room.

Sully is asleep. He sleeps like a toddler. Bum in the air. His arm wrapped around Red Ted, his stuffed bear he's had since he was a baby. She kisses his cheek. He smells like teenage boy, not like he should. Not like baby powder and diapers. More like body odour and bad breath.

She pulls away. He smells too much like a grown-up boy.

Somehow she gets through the kitchen where Angene and Chelsea are building some kind of sculpture out of grapes and hard-boiled eggs. The smell is unbearable. It smells like sickness, like something rotting.

The Jeep stalls. Won't start. She floods it and waits. Turns on the radio and tries to make herself calm down.

"Didn't happen," she tells herself in the mirror. "Doesn't matter."

The engine finally roars to life. She doesn't stop to pick up Aurelia like she always does. Aurelia can figure it out. She's mad at her, in a way that feels bigger than anything she can imagine. Maybe it's misplaced: this hatred should be focused only on Israel, but it's not. It's spreading. Infecting everything she's ever thought she cared about. It's Aurelia's laugh she keeps hearing. Aurelia's voice. Aurelia calling last night and denying she saw anything, claiming that she had no idea what happened until Matti told her. She was tobogganing with Jackson, she says. She was busy. She was stuck in a snowbank. She thought she was going to freeze to death down there, that she was actually going to die, and here Michael is, yelling at her, and that's not what friends do.

What friends do, thought Michael. She hung up the phone. Erased Aurelia from her speed dial.

Methodically erased all The Girls. None of them helped her. None of them were friends. Which she guesses she knew all along.

She woke up with Yale of all people asleep in the bed next to her. The door bolted. Keeping them out.

They all watched.

Michael breathes deeply. Yale will be at school. That steadies her a bit.

Her chest seizes again. She's gasping. Panicking. Someone is behind her, someone is looking over her shoulder, someone is watching her.

No, no. No one is there.

She pulls the car over to the side of the road and closes her eyes for a few minutes, working on the meditation chant that Hope says is miraculous. And it does clear her head. A bit. Only she's repeating in her head, "It didn't happen. It didn't happen. It didn't happen."

Only it did.

I'll just stop going to school, she thinks. *I'll do the rest by correspondence. I'll explain to a counsellor, but, no, she'll make me do something. "Press charges." I can hear it now. And that's never going to happen. Never. No way.* She won't go through that. Not a chance.

She turns the car around and drives home. She isn't ready.

She stands in the entrance to the house, listening. It's so busy in there. Her parents crashing around. Her sisters in the studio. Even upstairs, there is a racket. In Sully's room, she can hear the caregiver getting him dressed. Getting him ready for the day. She sits down in the hallway outside his room. Pries off her boots. They're pretty but they're so hard to get on and off. What is she waiting for? What is he getting ready for? Things like this would never happen to him, not just because he's a boy, but because he doesn't have to go through it. No one expects anything of him.

It isn't fair.

She closes her eyes, crawls down the hall to her room. It's like crawling is all she can do.

She'll go to school tomorrow. Face it all tomorrow. Not today. Today she has a headache. That's all. A migraine. Today she'll just close her eyes.

Yale

16

It's too much.

When I come home, Mum and Dad act like nothing has happened. They don't ask me where I've been. They don't wonder why my hands are shaking more than ever, like paper ribbons caught in a fan.

They don't notice that I'm different. How can they not notice?

I *am* different.

I don't know what I feel.

It's like all the smells are stuck to me. All that stench of fear. I'll never forget it. The tinny smell of blood and hot smell of sweat. The salty smell of pain. The white hot scent of anger.

Everything has a smell. Everything permeates.

I feel like my face should look different, transformed, even disfigured by the ugliness that I witnessed. But in the mirror, I'm still just me. Irregular freckles, wispy hair, dog eyes. The house is the same: it smells of curry and socks, dust litters the floor, unopened mail spills off the hall table. In the kitchen sink, three saucepans with macaroni crud in them make me feel that time has stood still. I want — I need — for there to be a shift, and I want it to be universal. For suddenly everything to be in Technicolor or black and white or to smell different or to feel different. The fact that it is all just the same — my parents are just the same — makes me angry in a way that I can't even pinpoint.

Nothing is different.

Everything should be different.

I guess I am what's different. What I did. I don't know. I never would ever have thought that I would be a person who did what I did. It makes me think of stories you hear where people will pull a cougar off a kid, or lift a car off a baby. Because in that moment, I felt like I could do that. Israel was the car. I lifted him off.

But did I? Not fast enough. The reality was that maybe I gave him a black eye, but I didn't stop him in time. Not before he started to do what he was going to do. Not before Michael was already really hurt.

I took too long.

What kind of superhero does that?

So I'm not a superhero. I'm just me. Tony might qualify. If he had been there instead of me, it wouldn't have got that far. The way he pounded Israel, I thought he was going to kill him. I wanted him to kill him. I will never forget the smirk on Israel's face. I think he really is a bad guy. And maybe, after all, Tony and I are both good guys. Maybe that's all there is to it.

I hope Michael is okay. I want to call her, to go to her house, to find out for sure. I need to know. It's like she's my responsibility and I have a right to know. But I don't call because I'm waiting for her to come to me. I think she will. I think maybe we'll really be friends now. But I also think it doesn't matter. It's like I've spent my whole life thinking she's so important and she's not really. She's just a girl.

I'm just a girl.

But maybe I'm also important.

I feel like I'm a part of so much all of a sudden that when I'm at home and Mum and Dad are ignoring me, robbing banks and eating children's food or whatever, I feel like I'm just on pause, waiting for more to happen.

Last night, I did something else that's changed me. I went down to the basketball court behind the old bowling alley. I went to see if Tony was there. There's something about him now that I can't stay away from. It's like everyone else from the scene has faded away and it comes down to me and Tony, Michael and Israel. The important players.

He wasn't there. Not right away. So I waited. I sat there for quite a while with the homeless guy, but not *with* him. We didn't talk, but even though I was invisible, he knew I was there. He kept looking at me. I was testing him, to be honest. I'm pretty sure he's the only one who can see me when I'm gone and I'm dying to know why. What extra vision does he have? Is it because he's mentally ill, something extra making up for whatever he has lost?

He watched me and muttered. I wonder what's wrong with him, but whatever it is, it's too far gone to fix. Maybe he doesn't want it to be fixed. Maybe he likes his life the way it is; how can I know? Anyway, I can't rescue him and he doesn't want rescuing, even if I knew how. I can tell that by the way his face is set, the lines making rivulets in his dry skin. His eyes fixed and steady even though they are bloodshot and leaking. He's not looking for help.

Then, finally, long after it got cold, Tony came. He appeared out of nowhere almost like I willed him to do it. I could smell him before I could see him. I could smell the dirt-sweat smell of him. He was bouncing on his feet, like he couldn't stay still, but it wasn't a happy kind of restless. His anger and frustration were everywhere. He was moving around like he was on a chain he couldn't break free from.

Then, of all people, Israel showed up. I thought there would be a fight. Tony's fists clenched under all the white tape. But there wasn't.

And then it got stranger.

Well.

I waited. I watched. I wanted to stop him from taking the bottle but I didn't. It felt like it wasn't my business somehow. Who was I to change his choice, right? It was his call. I felt bad about it, yet I couldn't bring myself to interfere. Even though I knew it wouldn't go well for him. I knew.

Some kind of hero I turned out to be. I let him do it. Let him keep drinking and drinking. I could have stopped him simply by appearing, but I didn't. I watched.

Like some kind of creepy voyeur.

Just sat there.

All night, literally, Tony drank and drank. The bum seemed to have a stash of bottles, I never would have guessed that he had a supply. The smell of whatever was hidden by the brown paper bag burned my nose. I don't know what it was. Couldn't see a label. There's another smell I'll never forget. Like medicine and fertilizer and some harsh stinging metal. Tony winced every time he swallowed. He was talking a lot. About his brother. The bum didn't even pretend to listen. Just kept swigging himself until he passed out. Maybe he is mute; I've never heard him speak.

But that didn't stop Tony. He kept talking. He talked about how when Joe died, Israel became his brother, sort of, in exchange. He talked about how he'll never speak to Israel again. He cried a bit. There was something about Michael that I didn't catch. I think he might have said something about me, but right then I was at a distance, under the maple tree and I might have heard it wrong. I had to walk away a few times. To pee, obviously. But also to breathe.

It was intense.

Maybe I should have stopped him, after all. It's just … he didn't seem to need help until he slumped over. When he tipped and passed out, I was scared. I thought he was dead. But he was moving, he was still drinking. Nursing the bottle like a baby. I was scared he'd drink so much he'd die so I finally took it away, reached out and touched it and it vanished. I threw it into the night and it splintered hard and loud on the concrete.

The homeless guy shifted in his sleep, his snoring — which I hadn't noticed until it stopped — abating and then beginning again in earnest.

Tony was definitely unconscious. I rocked back and forth, hugging my knees. What could I do? Call 911? I looked close, so close I could feel his breath on my face. He was breathing deeply, evenly. The smell of it made me reel.

Then he came to, suddenly, startled me into visibility. I couldn't stop it, it was like I was reappearing in spite of myself. He fished around for the bottle and not finding it, he started to talk. To me, or so it looked. He stared right at me. Talking, talking. I felt like I shouldn't be there, it was too personal, but I also couldn't leave. I couldn't leave him alone. He talked more. Mostly about his mum and his dad. Still more about Joe. I think he said, "I knew you'd understand, I could tell that you'd get it."

He held my hand. Not romantically, not really, more like someone who needed some help crossing the street.

I waited it out. I waited until I made sure he was awake, just in case. I don't know in case of what. Just in case. Finally he slept, and then woke up in the dawn light. Dazed and looking like he was in agony. Terrible. I wanted to hug him, but instead I vanished before he could be reminded that I was there and that maybe he had said more than he wanted to say. I think that was why, anyway. I just knew I had to do it, for his sake, to protect him, I guess, from feeling embarrassed in the cold light of day.

On my way home, I stopped at Michael's. It's not so much that I have to look after her, it's just that I wanted to make sure. They never lock their door. I don't know why not. I guess they know that any burglar would be so startled by the mausoleum of dead animals that he'd turn tail and run. They didn't bother me anymore; I was almost used to them. I waited in the front hall until I was sure the house was quiet. Everyone was still asleep. I could tell by the way the air smelled, like sleep punctuated with the sour air of a house that wasn't being moved through.

I made my way up to Sully's room first. He was sound asleep, arms flung over his head like he was being held at gunpoint. Snuck into his closet, perched there on his mountain of shoes. I was just watching him for a minute, lost in a daydream of Yale, when suddenly there was someone in the room with him, an aide I guess. Some kind of paid help I hadn't seen before, who was helping him to get dressed. The closet door opened and closed, but not all the way, and even though it felt wrong I found myself watching him being dressed. It's not that I wanted to see him undressed, nothing like that. It just made me feel so close to him, I almost cried. I know he's not Yale. They're nothing alike. He's a boy, for one thing. Plus he's not related to me.

I made myself leave the room; the door was partially ajar, enough for me to squeeze through. The now-familiar hallway with the odd crunchy carpet. Then, before I could go farther, Michael was there. For a minute, I thought she saw me. She was right next to me, walking from the direction of the stairs, and then she dropped to the floor and crawled to her room. I think she was crying.

I felt a million things. Sorry for her. Guilty that I hadn't stopped it sooner. Bad that I hadn't called her, after all, hadn't found out how she was doing.

I went straight home. I know I was supposed to be at school. But who cared? It was like being invisible made me immune to all that.

I went up to my room and I called her.

I said, "I just wanted to, you know, see if you were okay."

TONY

17

IT'S LIKE THE world has gone fucking insane, that's what it's like. I can't even believe any of this is happening.

The whole school is talking about the ski trip, and, believe me, they aren't talking about the slopes. They're talking about what happened. Well, of course they are. In that stupid way that happens, where everyone is all, "I was there! I saw it!" when I know that wasn't true because when it was really happening it was just Israel and Michael and Yale and finally, too late, me. The crowd only gathered afterward, they were drunk and stupid, they didn't even know what they were seeing. Which makes the whole thing even more sickening, how they are talking about Michael like she *deserved* it. Like what Israel did was what she had coming. Are they *sick*?

They have to be. They must be. Even her friends. Especially her friends. Like they've been lying in wait for this moment so they can make the pretty girl pay the price for being pretty. It's fucking disgraceful, that's what it is. Inhuman.

And I'm a bad guy, too. My broken knuckles throb and the pain shoots all the way through to my chest, which aches. *I'm* a bad guy — according to the rumour mill, anyway — for hurting Israel. Apparently, I broke his ribs.

Well, too fucking bad.

I'm the bad guy?

Well, fuck everyone. They have no idea. They're just siding with what must look, to them, like the winning team. They don't understand at all. It's all wrong.

To top it off, I'm sick. I'm *so* sick. I have to keep going into the bathroom to puke, and when I'm in there I'm treated to a big black-lettered graffiti drawing of Michael on her knees sucking some guy's dick, a big sign around her neck saying, I'M A SLUT.

People are disgusting. And cruel. For some reason, this makes me think of Joe. Maybe that's all he could see, you know? The cruelty. The nastiness. Maybe that's why he had to go because once you've seen that, it's hard to carry on. The truth of that makes me dizzy. I'm dizzy, anyway, but it's not just that. It's beyond distasteful. It's almost as bad as the thing itself. Evil.

I hope she presses charges. I hope that asshole goes to jail.

I puke and I puke and I puke. Above the flusher, someone has written, FOR A GOOD TIME CALL ——. It's Michael's real number, too. I spend ages rubbing at it with my finger until it's faded enough to not show that much. My knees on the cold tile floor, the stink of my own puke making me sick some more.

The stink. Everything stinks. *I* stink. Yeah, it's a hang-over so I guess you could say it's self-inflicted, which it is.

So this, I guess, I deserve. But no one would probably guess that I got it not from partying but from drunkenly pouring out my soul to a homeless guy on a glass-flecked concrete basketball court.

God.

I'm disgusting.

How did I get like this? Each time I catch a glimpse of myself, I newly hate me. I see Israel in passing and ignore him. His *swagger*. Is he actually proud of himself? Who the fuck *is* he, anyway? Not who I thought, that's for sure. Not anyone I could have ever known.

My jaw is clenched so tight, I feel like my eyes might pop out.

I can't stand anything. I'm crawling out of my skin.

The only person at the moment who I actually want to see is Yale. But she isn't at school. Neither is Michael.

I think I have to find Yale. I have to leave this horrible place and find her. See her. I have to explain to her how I feel. I know it's bad timing, probably, and might come out all wrong especially in the context of what happened, but suddenly it's like it's *urgent* that she know that I like her. I have to tell her. Even though I'm gross and I stink and I look terrible, all hollow-eyed and green. I have to know how she feels. I think — and I could be totally wrong — the way she was looking at me on that endless bus trip home, that there was something there for her, too. I want to make sure she's okay, but it's not just that. I just want to see how she's going to look at me and see from there if I'm safe to tell her how I feel. I've never ever felt this way before. It's like one good thing in a sea of bad things that are going on and I don't know what else to do with it other than just tell her. I don't give a shit what anyone else thinks anymore. Everything is so crazy. I feel like she's the only non-crazy person in the whole mess.

Michael

18

Michael lies in her bed. Her perfect clothes are sweaty under the heavy quilt. The air smells unwashed. The house sounds thump around her. A while ago, her mum came in. Laid her cool hand on Michael's forehead. Brought her an Aspirin, which Michael dutifully swallowed. Like an *Aspirin* could fix everything. She did have pain. Pain she'd never admit to. Like real physical pain, not just the pain in her mind. Pain from the sex mostly. A strange cramping in her abdomen. A feeling like she's been sitting on blades. She's bleeding.

She lies there and feels the trickle. The taste of the partly dissolved Aspirin in her mouth. She could never swallow pills. She watches the sunlight make patches of brightness on the white ceiling. The peach tree outside her window occasionally caressing the glass with a lazy branch. The blue sky peeking through the slats of the blinds. She picks up a book, but doesn't open it. She hardly ever reads and she can't concentrate now but it seems important to have something in her hand. Then it feels too heavy, so she drops it on the floor. Every noise she makes feels too loud. The slap of the book onto the hardwood. The heavy thud of the quilt following as she pushes it off, suddenly feeling like it's squashing her. Suffocating her.

The phone rings. She isn't going to pick it up but then she does, mostly to make the sound stop.

"Hello."

"Michael?"

"Who is this? What do you want?"

"It's ... Yale."

"Oh," she says. "That's okay. I mean, thanks."

"I just wanted to, you know, see if you were okay," Yale says.

"I'm okay," Michael says. Then she bursts into tears. Real tears. Like an unstoppable downpour of rain. Her sweater front is soaked.

"I'm coming over," Yale says finally.

"Okay," Michael says.

She gets out of bed. Changes into a clean T-shirt and sweats. Goes into the bathroom and washes off her makeup. Pulls her hair back into a ponytail. Cleans herself again. She can't get clean enough. While she waits for Yale, she cleans the bathroom floor. She cleans the toilet. She cleans her teeth.

Then Yale is there. At first, it's awkward. They're obviously both thinking about the same thing. How can they not be? Michael suddenly, more than anything, wants her to leave. She wants to be alone. Yale is too much of a real person, she sees that now. Yale is too human. Yale is ... Yale saw what happened to her, so she can't pretend differently. In light of this, people like Madison, like Aurelia, like Sam — people like them who are so fake, so surface — are maybe easier to take.

But Yale doesn't leave. She sits down on Michael's bed like it's her own, even though she doesn't look quite comfortable. Her eyes look nervous. Her hands are shaking.

"Your hands are shaking," Michael says.

"I know," says Yale. "They always do. It's not that I'm nervous or something. It's not that."

"Oh," says Michael.

Even that short burst of conversation feels like a lot. She crawls onto the bed herself. Curls up at the end like a cat. When she was little, she had a stuffed tiger that lay there (an actual toy, not a real stuffed cat), just like she's lying now, head on her paws, like her head is too heavy to lift. She wants to close her eyes.

"Maybe I'm nervous," says Yale. "I think I'm always nervous."

Michael doesn't answer. Yale's shoes are dirty and clods of dirt have fallen onto the hardwood floor, onto Michael's quilt. The dirt bothers Michael more than she can say, so she doesn't say anything because anything she says about it would come out wrong. Instead, she closes her eyes. Pretends she can't feel the stinging between her legs. Pretends that Yale being there isn't taking her back to the moment itself, again and again and again.

"I'm really sorry," says Yale, suddenly. "I was there, I should have stopped him sooner, I should have … I'm so sorry."

Michael's eyes are startled open. "What do you mean?" she says.

"I should have stopped him before," she says again. "I should have."

"Oh," says Michael. She hadn't thought of that. It wasn't Yale's responsibility. "You didn't have to do anything," says Michael. "I've never done anything for you."

"It's not like that," says Yale. "It's not like, I'll do this if you do that. It's like, I don't know, someone's in trouble, so you help them no matter what."

"I don't want to talk about it," Michael whispers. "I'm just home because I have a migraine."

Yale cocks her head to one side. "I get those, too," she says.

"I get sick," says Michael. "I get so I can't see."

"Me too," says Yale.

"It sucks," says Michael.

"I know," says Yale. "It's the worst."

The silence is awkward, but it's not really silent. The house is alive with sounds. Music reverberates from the living room–studio where the sisters are finishing the last of their photos for their upcoming show. Sully thumps on the wall in rhythm with a song only he can hear. The music therapist is in there with him and suddenly she bursts into a rendition of "The Sound of Music" at full volume that makes Yale and Michael laugh. It isn't really funny, but the laughing feels like exhaling.

"Okay," says Michael. "I think I'm going to sleep now."

"Do you want me to go?" says Yale.

"No," says Michael. "Stay."

She closes her eyes. Stretches out enough that just a part of her leg touches Yale's. That's all. So that she's not quite alone, after all.

Yale

19

I walk home from Michael's house slowly. My legs are
sore from lying down in such an awkward position but I
also feel somehow lighter. I pass a tree that's in full blos-
som and it's swarming with bees, their hum feels like it's
coming from inside me. If I hadn't gone, it would have
felt like a furious buzz of guilt. But I did go, and it was
okay. I think she was glad to see me.

Actually, I know she was glad to see me.

Michael's going to go back to school tomorrow; she'll
pick me up on the way. We'll go in together, The Bleeder
and The Slut, heads held high. And what does it matter,
anyway? Six weeks from now this school year will be over
and no one will remember either of our traumas, except
maybe some vague whispers at the reunion, which we
won't go to, anyway. Who really wants to see these people
again? I know I don't.

That's the thing, right? Everyone is so caught up in themselves that this won't seem so important to anyone else except
Michael, and me, in a week, a month, a year.

I'm walking. For the first time in ages, I don't feel like I want to disappear. I'm just breathing. The air brushes by my skin like a cat, soft. Spring is getting warmer and summer is hovering on the edge. You can smell it in the warm sidewalk smell and the patchy grass that's cropping up on lawns. Dandelions are everywhere and the slightly acrid odour they make when they are crushed is interspersed with the other, still-fresh smells of spring.

I'm almost home when I see Tony. He's standing on the sidewalk outside my house, spinning a basketball on his fingers again and again and again.

He's waiting for me.

"Hey," he says.

"Hey," I say.

At first, it's so awkward I want to die. Like we're circling each other, sniffing like dogs, trying to identify one another. We're not really sniffing, but you know what I mean. Then it feels like the square of concrete we're standing on is rotating us around, saying, "Look, see, this is who it is."

He looks embarrassed and I feel embarrassed. To hide my shaking hands, I stuff them into my jean pockets. It's like outside of the context of that night, we don't know each other at all. But still, when I look at his face, I *know* him. Like he's someone I knew a long time ago from somewhere and have only finally recognized.

"You know," he says. "You know ... So ..."

"What?" I say.

"Um," he says. He kind of shifts back and forth and the ball rolls out of his hand and onto the lawn. He looks like he wants to get it, but he doesn't. He stays put. I feel a bit sorry for him. It's like without a prop — a basketball, a pen — he doesn't know what to do with his hands. He settles on stuffing them deep into his pockets, mirroring me.

"I just wanted to tell you," he says. "I have to tell you, that what happened to you before ... You know, the thing. What happened to you. It was really stupid. I mean, not stupid that it happened. But what went on afterward. You didn't deserve that."

"Oh," I say. "Yeah. It was beyond. Beyond *beyond*."

"Yeah," he says. "Well, it was stupid. People suck. Like they have to laugh at someone else to turn the attention away from themselves, you know? I just wanted you to know that it didn't make me like you any less. It didn't, you know, change you."

The last part comes out in a burst. Like he's been rehearsing. I'm surprised. I couldn't be more surprised. My toes curl under.

"And the thing is," he says. "The thing is that I've always ... I mean, I do now. I like you. And I was wondering, if it weren't too weird, if you wanted to ..."

The whole world is standing still. If there were birds flying by, I'm sure they've frozen in time, dropped onto the lawn. I look up half-expecting it to start raining feathers. I can't breathe. I'm holding my breath.

I'm getting dizzy from it.

This is beyond surreal, so far beyond that I feel like I must be asleep or dead and this isn't happening, it's a hallucination. His arms dangle so awkwardly at his sides, he looks like he's in pain, like he's going to explode from it.

So all I do is just reach out my hand to him, and we stand like that for a long time. Just there, on the sidewalk outside my house, cars going by. A bus. A group of men on bicycles all wearing bright yellow and black outfits like a swarm of African killer bees.

My heart is going crazy, but I stay really still because that's what feels important. When I'm holding his hand, my hands don't shake. It's the weirdest thing. Finally, the wind picks up and my hair starts whipping around my face, and that kind of breaks the moment.

"So," he says.

"Yeah," I say. "Let's sit down."

We go sit on the lawn, which needs cutting. It's peppered all over with white daisies and thousands and thousands of bright yellow nodding dandelion heads. I sneeze four times in a row and then stop.

While we sit, and talk, he keeps crunching blades of grass between his fingers and rubbing them and from now on that smell will always be the best smell in the world for me.

TONY

20

YALE IS MY girlfriend. She's my girl. Mine.

I've been smiling a lot. In spite of everything. I'm still upset. Who wouldn't be? I'm torn up about Israel. Michael. Everything.

But something is shifting, somehow I can't explain. I know Yale is going away to school in the fall and so am I. It's not like happily ever after. Does that even exist? There is always an after.

But I don't care right now. Right now I care about the way she looks at me. The way I feel. The way I get to kiss her. The way she reaches out and touches my face. The way she somehow makes things okay.

That's the best part.

I can't explain it, but it's like *I'm* okay. Now. I was not okay for a long time, but something intangible has changed enough that now everything fits. I don't feel like I'm screwing everything up.

I don't feel like everything is my fault.

I don't even know what one thing altered that feeling, not really. Some kind of internal tide change, I guess. And I know it has to do with Yale. It has to do with how she knows everything there is to know about me and she still seems okay with me. With who I am. It has a lot to do with that.

Michael

21

School is ending. Michael isn't going to the prom. She doesn't want to go. She not only isn't going but she's given the dress away to a charity. She bought the dress last year. It was expensive. It was so long ago she barely remembers how much she loved it. It was from when she was a different person. And she's not skipping the whole event because she's depressed, even though maybe it's partly that. She's skipping it because she's already past it. She's thinking about what's after that and what's next, and prom is just a reminder of what's past.

Not interested.

It's been over a month. She doesn't hurt, physically. She isn't raw. There are no physical reminders, except maybe a sharp shock when she sits, like a phantom pain that she's read that people get after they have a limb removed. A pain in something that isn't there anymore.

She's okay. She is not okay. Or she thinks she is okay. She hopes she will someday be okay even though today isn't the day. Today is a bad day. She wishes — more than anything — that she could stop replaying the scene in her head and willing it to be different. She wishes that she …

She isn't okay, but if she decides that she will be, then she will be. She can't think any other way because to think any other way would be to let Israel take more than he already took. And that was enough.

She doesn't miss The Girls at all. It's easier now. She isn't trying so hard. It's just her and Yale. And Tony, of course. Yale and Tony are so easy together that it makes something ache inside her to see them together.

She's out with Yale, alone, hiking. Something she never thought she'd do. They've climbed up the side of a hill that's affectionately called a mountain even though it probably doesn't really fit the description. It's sunny, hot, both girls are sweating. The sky is an unrelenting shade of blue and her eyes squint even from their shaded perch behind her DKNY sunglasses (olive frames, dark lenses, so huge they cover almost her entire face). The path is rutted and uneven under their feet.

The wildflowers are blooming. So much colour. Dazzling, even through her tinted lenses. The flowers are making Yale sneeze, which she does every few metres, her whole body lurching like she's getting whiplash each time. Michael laughs in spite of herself. As it turns out, Yale is funny. She never would have thought that. Yale sneezes again and jumps straight into the air, ending the sneeze with a round-off. Bows.

"You can take something for that, you know," observes Michael. "Like allergy medicine?"

Yale shrugs. "I don't like drugs." She sneezes again.

"Loser," says Michael, but she says it affectionately.

She feels in some ways like she's been friends with Yale forever. She feels almost entirely relaxed. Almost. A part of her never relaxes. A part of her is always looking back over her shoulder, waiting. A part of her is braced for awfulness.

A breeze pushes through the grass on the west side of the trail, flattening it long enough for the girls to see two deer, eyes wide open, staring back at them. Yale sneezes again and the deer lift into the air, bounding out of sight into the trees.

"I've never seen a live one before," says Michael. "Isn't that weird?"

"It's not only weird," says Yale, "it's creepy. Don't all those dead animals freak you out?"

"Yes," says Michael. "You have no idea."

"I'd be having nightmares," says Yale.

"Yeah," says Michael. "Who wouldn't?"

"I wonder how Sully feels," Yale says. "I wonder if they scare him, too."

Michael stops walking. "I don't know," she says. "You know, I never much thought about it. I don't think so. I don't think he notices them so much. He's more detail oriented. He likes the glass eyes."

"Oh," says Yale.

They keep walking. Feet crunching on gravel that gives way to dirt and then becomes grass and moss. The moss hushes their footsteps so that Michael becomes more aware of her breathing, the sound it makes in the air. The trees shade them a bit from the sun and suddenly she's cold. She puts on a sweater from her pack, even though Yale is still sweating. It's like any temperature change is impossible for her now. She's more sensitive. Too sensitive.

Out of the blue, Yale starts to talk. Michael can't see her face because she's slightly ahead on the path, talking away from Michael but her voice being carried back.

"I have a sister," says Yale, and then she tells her. After a while, she's so outside of herself, anyway, that she feels like she's watching a movie or reading a novel. A story that's happening around her, not to her. Which is better than being involved.

Sort of.

Someone else's sadness feels safer to her than her own, and Yale sounds sad. Well, who wouldn't? Michael had thought her own parents were bad but Yale's sound downright insane.

Yale keeps talking as they scrabble over some boulders to get to the top. Michael trips, skins her knee, but she doesn't interrupt. The wound stings and bleeds.

They get to the top and sit down, the view spread out all around them like fabric. Michael lies back on the sun-warmed rock, pressing the sleeve of her Diesel sweater onto her cut so it stops bleeding. She turns her cheek into the ground, which is gravelly and scratches her skin.

Yale is making some connection between her disabled sister, whose name weirdly enough is also Yale, and Sully.

"Sully's not like that," says Michael automatically. "He's not crippled. He's just different."

"I know," says Yale. Finally stopping talking. Looking at Michael lying on the ground. Then more quietly, "You're lucky."

"Sorry," says Michael after a pause. "It's just that I'm always explaining about Sully."

"I don't know why I'm telling you," says Yale. "I kind of thought you'd get it."

"I do," says Michael. "I get it."

"Okay," says Yale. She sits down beside Michael. Kicks off her shoes, peels off her socks, digs her bare toes into the ground. Her toenails are painted bright green.

"I love the smell of it up here," says Yale. "It's so ... unpolluted."

"It's really fucked-up that they gave her the same name," Michael says suddenly. "It's like you almost don't exist."

Yale looks at her. "Thanks a lot," she says.

"I'm sorry," says Michael. "It's not coming out right. It's like they didn't give you your own identity, you know? Your own tag."

"I guess," says Yale. "I do feel ... well, it's stupid. I feel like I'm supposed to make up for her or something."

"You should change your name," says Michael. "Make up your own."

Yale shrugs. "I don't know," she says. "Maybe I don't mind it."

"I'm going to call you Y," says Michael. "Just to distinguish. Besides, it's mysterious. Y."

"Okay," says Yale. "Maybe."

"Anyway," Michael says. "Where is she?"

"I don't really know," confesses Yale. "I know the name of the place where they keep her but I don't even know what city it's in. It might not even be *here*."

"We can find it, Y," says Michael. "On the internet. How hard can it be?"

"Yes," says Yale. "I guess we can."

They slowly make their way back down the hill. It's getting cool in the afternoon, the clouds lazily drifting over the sun. When they get back to Michael's house, they go straight to the computer and enter the hospital name that Yale has memorized. Four of them are listed, four hospitals with the same name. It's not that hard, though — Michael is right — to figure out which one it must be. It takes less than an hour, eliminating the obvious.

It's not that far away. Yale hasn't disappeared at all. All this time, she's been right there. Just a couple of hours' drive north. She's been right there all along.

Yale

22

On our way to see Yale, we stopped at my house. I wanted Mum and Dad to ask where I was going so I could tell them, but they didn't come up from downstairs. The kitchen was such a mess, I was embarrassed that Michael saw it. What would she think? An open carton of eggs, the peanut butter jar with a spoon sticking out of it in the middle of the table, containers of day-old Chinese food making the whole place smell like the seeping ooze of a garbage dump. She didn't seem to notice. I guess that isn't surprising. Why would she care about the state of my kitchen? She's still stuck in what happened; of course, she is. A month, six weeks, it's not that much time. I don't expect she'll just snap back to being happy, being free. How can she?

I grabbed a sweater from my room. A jacket. Some money. I led Michael back outside. And Tony was there.

Tony.

That fresh grass smell. Dirt. I'll never get tired of it, ever. And I don't care that it sounds like a cliché, when I see him, something inside me just lifts up. I feel like I don't deserve it, like it's something that was meant to happen to someone who isn't me, but I'll take it just the same.

He came with us. The three of us in Michael's red Jeep. Listening to music. Michael driving. The three of us like a team, a ragtag team, sure, but still a team. The trees slipping past the windows. The city vanishing behind us on the highway. Fast-food restaurant after fast-food restaurant giving way to farmers' fields and a handful of lakes. A gas station that looked like the last building on earth. It felt like we'd left the planet. Like we were hurtling toward something ethereal. Something huge.

But it wasn't like that. It wasn't fun and games. It wasn't a lark. It wasn't even all about me. I could smell the sweat rising off Michael, and her nervousness coming in waves, like tides washing in and out over her. It was happening less than it happened at first, in that first week (two weeks, three weeks) after it happened, but it still happened. It happened all along the drive. I could see it in the way her face would suddenly change colour, the white of her hands gripping the wheel. She was so scared, but of what? I can see the panic attacks coming over her but I haven't brought it up yet. (Maybe I will, soon, maybe I won't. I don't always know the right thing to do.) I guess I'm waiting for her to say something about it, maybe it's something she just wants to deal with alone. I reach over and touch her arm and she flinches so I pull away.

Sometimes I think that Tony must make her think of Israel. Of course he does. The three of us together must keep taking her back again and again to that scene. Sometimes I catch her shivering, like she's freezing, even though it's hot in the car. I wish I hadn't brought Tony if it's him that's inadvertently making her feel this way, but I couldn't help it. I needed him to be there, too.

The hospital is more like a big old house. A country house.

By the time we got there, visiting hours were over. But I went in. I went in the only way I could. I told them to wait in the car, and then I disappeared. It was hard though. Different than all the other times. I had to really try and, even then, it wasn't perfect. I was coming through in blotches. It took me a while to find Yale's room. It was so much like a hospital room, it took me by surprise. The exterior of the building was so home-like, but in here it was typical: a bed with rails, linoleum floors, equipment beeping. That unmistakable hospital smell.

I wish I could say that, when I walk in, Yale opens her eyes and sits up, but she doesn't. She is lying there, motionless. Asleep, I guess. I can hear her breathing, which is uneven, catches a bit on every inhalation.

I reappear because I don't have the strength to stay gone and to absorb the scene at the same time.

Yale.

I say it out loud. "Yale."

She doesn't blink or even turn her head. Nothing. No shift in her hiccupy breathing, no change in her demeanour. The silence behind the hum of the machines is completely overwhelming. It's like there is no one there, but I can see her. She's *there*.

"Yale," I say more sharply.

Nothing.

I know right at that moment that I'm not going to rescue her. I'm not going to take her away from here, transform her, give her some of my life for her own. Save her, and somehow by doing that save myself. What had I been thinking?

I start to cry. It isn't her fault. She is who she is, whoever that is. But none of this is how I imagined it to be. I make myself stop. If she's aware of me (is she?), I don't want to hurt her feelings. I don't want her to think she's not good enough for me.

"I'm your sister," I say.

It feels funny to say it. It feels untrue.

"I am," I insist, as if she's argued with me by not responding. "I am your sister. We have the same name and everything."

She is only barely there. Barely, barely. Her eyes blink, and then they are open but not looking at anything. One is brown. One is blue.

I get dizzy, nearly fall.

I don't know what I was expecting, but this isn't it. Not at all. I feel ripped off, and then I feel sick about it. I feel …

Her hand twitches. But that is all. Her face is … not like any face I've ever seen, not anything I recognize. (Why did I think I'd know her? That she'd be like me? Crazy.) It's so misshapen and contorted. Unformed in some ways, overly formed in others. She looks scary, and then I hate myself for being scared. Or disappointed. Or both.

Even though I am sitting right there, on her bed, feeling the smooth white cotton of her sheets, she can't see me. That's what hurts the most. She doesn't know how to look.

I sit there for a long time. I wonder what Michael and Tony are doing but I can't bring myself to leave. I want to say more but talking out loud feels dumb, too loud in the stillness of the room. Too intrusive.

Then I realize that there is something. Something about the way she smells. I put my face close. I breathe in the air from her exhalation. I sniff between her neck and shoulder.

She smells like me. She smells like pumpkin.

The lump in my throat is choking me. I want ... I need ...

I don't know.

I kiss her cheek. Her skin is freckled like mine, but not. It is also rough and red. Dry. She sighs, or seems to. It might just be a quirk of the machine. She is looking around, past me, through me, her eyes darting like fish in a bowl.

"I'm here," I say. "I'm *here*."

There is motion in the hallway. The door opens. I disappear but stay in the room. The shadows are getting long. A nurse comes in with a clatter of trays, talking on a phone that she hangs up when she sits down. She feeds Yale. It is really slow going. Yale opens and closes her mouth like a baby bird, sometimes getting food, sometimes not. The nurse is gentle and so patient. She reminds me of Michael with Sully, just the way she's looking at Yale, the way she's touching her hand. She talks to her the whole time, quietly, about stuff I wouldn't know how to begin to bring up. Stuff about her own life. Like she's thinking out loud. It seems so easy when she does it, not like the awkward blurting that I was doing.

I guess maybe I just don't know how to be with Yale. Not yet. Maybe I'll come back. I *will* come back. I'll have a chance to figure it out. She's my sister. This isn't like a one-shot deal where I need to figure it all out in just one quick visit. There's no Hollywood ending here.

My sister.

I'm unexpectedly sobbing again. Hard. It's not even that I'm sad; I'm just so full of emotion I can't figure out how to get it out other than tears. The nurse's kindness is tearing me open. I guess if that's what the money is buying, is it wrong?

The bank won't miss it.

I don't know what I feel. I swallow and swallow and try to stop. I feel so confused. I thought I was going to take her away with me. Take her home. Put her in front of Mum and Dad and make them look. Make them see her. But that obviously isn't going to happen. It was obviously a dumb, naïve idea.

But the thing is, something more than that has happened. Something else that's changed me. I've seen her. I've seen that she's okay. And it's kind of like I can exhale now, like I've been holding my breath since the moment I heard about her and now I've finally stopped.

I understand something suddenly that I didn't realize I needed to understand until just this minute: she's not me.

Yale is not me.

I wait for the nurse to go, and then I reappear and go say goodbye. I press my nose against her cheek, breathe deeply. I hold my own cheek against her face, just so maybe she can recognize me, too.

I walk back to the car slowly; through my shoes the grass feels softer than anything I've ever felt. I smoke one of my clove cigarettes. Exhale it out my nostrils so that it burns and hurts. The smell fills in everything. The air is so warm and it is dark, but in the sky there are millions of stars. Way more than you ever see in the city. The blackness is freckled with them, so many they look fake. They look like someone spilled a can of light. I sit down on a bench and finish my cigarette. I try to make my hand disappear, just because, but I can't.

I can't.

I feel like screaming at first, and then I feel like whooping at the sky. Like something has broken inside me, but that maybe it broke *right*. Something that had been waiting to break for a long time. Something that had been blocking me up and it hurt to remove it, but now it's stopped.

I am jittery with it. My hands, my trembling hands, are still the same but somehow the trembling looks less like fear and more like what I used to long for: feathers, fluttering. And it's from excitement. And also from nerves. It's like suddenly I realize that everything is just starting.

Everything.

It seems like a long time ago that I had a crush on Tony's *skin*. Now it's so much more than that. I want to unsee all the things about him that I saw that I shouldn't have seen, that he'll never know that I know until (if) he wants to talk about them to me.

After all, it wasn't mine to see in the first place.

I get back in the car, and from the backseat Tony says, "So?" And I shrug.

I say, "It's okay."

Michael says, "Are you sure?"

And I say, "Yes, I really am."

And it's true, I am. I am okay. We're all okay. Or okay enough for now, anyway. Even Yale, in her own way, is okay. Michael starts up the car and pulls out onto the road. Tony reaches through the seats and turns on the radio. His hand rests on my shoulder, lightly, so that I can barely feel it, and I turn my head so it rests against his skin. And that's that.

We head for home.

DON'T MISS THE NEXT AMAZING
TITLE IN THE XYZ TRILOGY ...

What Z Sees

Sometimes you have to listen to the voices in your head ...

MY WHOLE LIFE is different now. It's as though every key on the piano is being played at once. It's awful. It's both awful and incredible, if I'm being honest. It's easier to just think of it as awful, but it has a good side, too. I'm mesmerized by it, even though I also want it to stop.

This thing.

I was confused when I woke up in the hospital. I just thought that was normal. Everyone is confused when they come around after being unconscious, right? Only it didn't pass ...

I opened my eyes and I was in a room painted the colour of powdered lemonade, and all that stuff about "too bright" was too true ...

I wasn't alone for long before the curtain shifted and Maman appeared in her chair. Something was different though. She was different. At first, I didn't realize what I was seeing: a brightness around her so saturated it was like watching a colourful glass tile mosaic being thrown through the air, in slow-motion. She was thinking blurrily and I automatically read it, interpreted it: *My baby, my baby girl, ma jeune fille.* She was thinking, *thank God for this, that she's okay. I'll never ask for anything again.*

Oh no, I thought. *No no no.*

But that thought was interrupted by a nurse bustling in, blood pressure cuff in hand, chirping happily, How are we feeling? While thinking, *Two more and I can go home, if that pig hasn't eaten the whole pizza maybe I'll have some of that and take a bath. Maybe I'll eat it in the bath, have a glass of wine, paint my toenails, I never paint my nails anymore, I wonder when I stopped.*

Her sadness drifted around her like a mermaid's hair underwater, even while the whole time she smiled at me with artificially bright white teeth.

How could I be seeing that?

It was like seeing someone's thoughts through a fog, through glass covered with a film of steam. I couldn't help squinting through the blur. It was like I had to see it, a compulsion, I couldn't stop it …

I tried to think about songs. My song. I kept my eyes glued shut and repeated some lyrics over and over again in my head. My own lyrics. *Absolutely*, I repeated. *Absolutely feeling like I absolutely know. Absolutely everything and still I absolutely go.*

The words felt wrong though. I felt like I was thinking in someone else's language. I couldn't shake the feeling that I must be dying. Because somehow it felt almost celestial, to see everything. It felt surreal to be so disconnected from myself.

And it also felt like the worst thing in the world. It was so much. Too much …

Author's Note

What happens in this book is rape. I want to be really clear about it, because the character of Michael in this book does not necessarily make the choices afterwards that I would advocate. Rape is rape. No matter what you're wearing, no matter how much you've had to drink, no matter how much flirting has taken place, no matter what: if you have said "no," clearly and repeatedly, and someone doesn't stop, it's rape. Rape is a crime. It is not your fault when it happens, it's the rapist's fault. It is never okay.

Michael clearly said "no." Israel didn't stop. I wish this never happened, I wish "no" was enough, but it isn't always, and scenes like the one in this book are happening every day, all over North America and beyond. So what I ask of you is this: if you are thinking "no," say "no." Say, "I do not want this." Do not leave it unsaid or unclear. Do not ask yourself later if you really said "no." Do not leave the door open for second-guessing yourself. Do not let other people try to convince you that you didn't really, did you? And didn't you really want it, after all? Be true to yourself.

And if someone doesn't listen to "no" (and I sincerely hope this never happens to you), then press charges. Follow through. Let everyone know that this isn't okay. What often happens is that it becomes a secret. A shameful secret. And yet you — the victim, in this case — have no reason to be ashamed. You said "no." Someone didn't listen. And you have nothing to be ashamed of. *They* do. I hope you understand that, and I hope that if anything like this happens to anyone you know that you will stand beside them while they take the right path. Press charges. Tell people. Stand up for your right to say "no" and mean it and have it mean exactly that. *No.*

Check out my website, **karenrivers.com**, where I've posted links to some great rape-support websites that offer much better advice than I can.

Please.

By printing Y in the Shadows on paper made from 100% recycled fibre (40% post-consumer recycled) rather than virgin tree fibre, Raincoast Books has made the following ecological savings:

- 85 trees
- 3,382 kilograms of greenhouse gases (equivalent to driving an average North American car for over six months)
- 59 million BTUs (equivalent to the power consumption of a North American home over six months)
- 117,140 litres of water
- 1,803 kilograms of solid waste

Environmental savings were estimated with the Environmental Defense Paper Calculator. For more information, visit www.papercalculator.org.

RAINCOAST BOOKS
www.raincoast.com

ANCIENT FOREST
FRIENDLY

KAREN RIVERS has published nine previous young adult and juvenile books, including *Surviving Sam*, which was nominated for the 2004 White Pine Award, and the Haley Andromeda trilogy (*The Healing Time of Hickeys*, *The Cure for Crushes*, *The Quirky Girls' Guide to Rest Stops and Road Trips*). *The Healing Time of Hickeys* was nominated for the 2003 Canadian Library Association's "Young Adult Book of the Year" award, is a Children's Book Centre Our Choice selection and was a featured title for Barnes & Noble and Amazon.ca.

Karen lives in Victoria, British Columbia.